W9-AQP-418

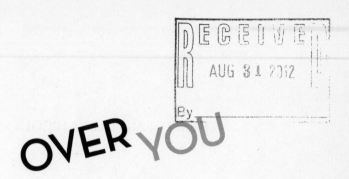

OVER YOU

EMMA McLAUGHLIN
AND
NICOLA KRAUS

HARPER TEEN

An Imprint of HarperCollins*Publishers*

HarperTeen is an imprint of HarperCollins Publishers.

Over You
Copyright © 2012 by Emma McLaughlin & Nicola Kraus
All rights reserved. Printed in the United States of America.
No part of this book may be used or reproduced in any manner
whatsoever without written permission except in the case of brief
quotations embodied in critical articles and reviews. For information
address HarperCollins Children's Books, a division of HarperCollins
Publishers, 10 East 53rd Street, New York, NY 10022.
www.epicreads.com

Library of Congress Cataloging-in-Publication Data is available.
ISBN 978-0-06-172043-7

Typography by Andrea Vandergrift
12 13 14 15 16   LP/RRDH   10 9 8 7 6 5 4 3 2 1
❖
First Edition

*To all the guys who broke our hearts—we wouldn't appreciate
what we have today without you*

"Rejection is the greatest aphrodisiac."
—*Proust as quoted by Madonna*

CHAPTER 1

An early fall leaf loosens from a tree and blows into Max's jacket, fluttering down and getting crushed beneath the toe of her platform pump as she strides down the sidewalk purposefully to her next case.

By seventeen, Max Scott has created so many versions of herself she's almost lost count—but *this* is the one she loves best. Previously Max always readily adapted to the style norms of whatever new school she transferred into. And she transferred a lot. As the only child of a single mother, Max had to move whenever her mom's latest journalism job folded with the local paper. From

Denver to Daytona. Another furniture set from USA Rentals, another faux granite kitchenette, another stack of boxes that wouldn't get unpacked.

While none of it would have been her first choice, even Max had to admit it had made her into a keen observer of the human animal.

Here's who Max was not: that new girl who slunked in the corner with her hands tucked into her sleeves waiting for a vampire to find her irresistible. She did not abide furtive glances and chewed bottom lips. And she would seriously rather be found dead than staring into her lunch tray at a table in Cafeteria Siberia. Please.

Over the years Max developed a system. When it came to being the new girl, Max learned to get herself to the mall. She would set up camp at the food court's Cold Stone Creamery or enticing equivalent and then covertly watch as most girls passed with envious eyes and snide comments. It was the girls who stopped and ordered a big group-something to share, who dug in while talking each other's ears off, laughing so hard they sprayed whipped cream, pecan frosting, or pretzel crumbs, that caught Max's attention. There was nothing Max valued more than those who found the funny.

Once she spotted them, Max watched, listened, recorded, and then Google cross-referenced so by the first day of school she had their look down with just enough variation so as not to appear to be "trying." Max's system helped her to find her peeps pronto, and she didn't care what brand pants they wore so much as that they could crack up until they wet them.

Thus one year there was an athletic, ponytailed version of Max who wore sneakers and said "hey" instead of "hello." In Cincinnati, there was a version who wore leggings for so many months she had permanent seam indentations running up her thighs. There was an eighth-grade version who wore heavy black eyeliner and wasn't easily impressed. A version who wore teal eyeliner and clapped twice in exuberance upon discovering Pizza Day. One who played with American Girl dolls (fourth grade), and one who gave them buzz cuts (fifth grade). At this point, so as not to confuse the friends she'd picked up along the way, her Facebook photo was Audrey Hepburn in a cocktail dress fashioned from a bedsheet from *Breakfast at Tiffany's*—hewing closest to Max's authentic ideal. Max believed style and wit equipped a girl to best nearly anything.

Nearly.

Max had embraced each new school. And she had always been embraced back. That was until her parents decided Max should attend one place consecutively for her junior and senior years to ensure a smooth transition to the caliber of college they hoped for her. So they packed Max off to a rigid—read: humorless—New England boarding school, the kind with a chapel, a crest, and a Latin motto. The thought of it still makes her cringe. And into this vacuum of funny, this vortex of blah and bland, stepped *him*. The one. The answer. The reason. Hugo Tillman.

Hugo made her feel seen, he made her feel loved, he got her jokes and her style. And then the thing happened that happens at some point to every girl, in every school in the world. Max was informed that he who she loved most was no longer in love with her. Max Scott was dumped.

With a few slicing words from Hugo, her life came crashing in. And with no "home" to go to, she settled for the next-best thing—heading to her mother's latest mailing address: New York City, where Max found the inspiration to channel her roiling misery.

Refusing to return to school, any school, period, Max spent the rest of what would have been her junior year walking the mazelike halls of the Metropolitan Museum of Art, where she was drawn to the doleful eyes of a nineteenth-century black-and-white photograph. The eyes looked exactly like the ones staring hollowly back at Max in the medicine-cabinet mirror every morning. Camille Claudel, Rodin's mistress and muse. She'd inspired him, informing the sculpting style that would make him world famous forever, and he, by way of thanks, dumped her ass, stole her technique, and locked her up in an insane asylum when she tried to speak of it.

From there Max roamed the twentieth-century galleries, with their low lighting, low ceilings, and tiger wood walls. The squeaking snow boots she'd been living in called the passing attention of the sparse tourists, but she didn't care. She was too busy contemplating the O'Keeffes. Along with the naked photographs taken by Georgia's partner, Alfred Stieglitz. The very photos that garnered *him* renown and recognition prevented Georgia's peers from taking her work seriously in her lifetime. Now everyone gets that posing naked is not the route to respect, but how was Georgia to know? She was just making Alfred happy.

Max looped through that wing toward the ornate portraits of Henry VIII's beheaded wives, their only crime that they accepted his proposal of marriage. Then on to the Greek vases, where goddesses and mortals alike prostrate themselves over hearts broken by callous gods. She spotted Daphne, Io, and Persephone, for whom male attention brought agony and destruction.

She sat for hours on a bench across from a painting of Cleopatra committing suicide. *How?* she asked herself. How is it that civilization evolved the ability to shuttle someone to the moon, but other than capturing its excruciating details in every medium, it hadn't come up with anything to guide women through heartbreak? Max walked past the first thermometer, the first coins. *Girls have no tools, no systems at our disposal,* Max thought. *Turning ourselves into trees is frankly a crap suggestion—thanks, Greeks.*

Because, let's face it, Rodin went on to wealth and glory, Zeus went on to turn another goddess into a hamster or a barn door or whatever, Henry handed those wives in at the gallows like he was getting a rebate at a car dealership and got to start his own religion. The guys took and still take hearts with impunity and are fine. *More than fine, they have fame and fortune and empires. They still hook up. They still play Wii. And we? We?*

Max caught sight of herself in the glass shielding Ophelia from the light. *I am scary thin,* she thought. *I have eggplant circles under my eyes. I want to play Wii. Or at least want to want to play Wii. It's been* centuries. *We cannot still be incurring the blow of rejection with as little at our disposal as Cleopatra. Civilization has come up with cars and nuclear power plants, Blu-ray movies, open-heart surgery, and Cesar Millan. There has to be a way to evolve this. I will evolve this,* Max thought.

And so she has. A few months later she is her favorite version of herself, which, in her carriage and comportment, in her choice of dress and words, exudes the confidence of a girl who feels herself to be precisely where she ought to be. No one would guess, as they admiringly watch her stride down the asphalt to wherever she is needed next, that this confidence is extremely hard won.

Under the navy night sky, Max checks the address texted to her and walks a few paces down to the appointed stoop on Bank Street, the one lined with carved pumpkins. She drops her BlackBerry back into her hard-sided red bag, jogs up the steps, and rings the bell, smoothing her tight, black skirt suit and reviewing in her mind the details of the particular tragedy awaiting her. She notes that the large living room window is pasted with construction-paper bat cutouts. Which confirms her instinct that there are younger siblings on the premises. As the door is unlocked, Max can smell the Old El Paso taco dinner that's long since been cleared from the table.

"Hello?" A woman with bare feet below her trousers stands rubbing her hands dry on a dishcloth.

"Hi! Mrs. Stetson? I'm Max. I'm here to see Bridget."

"The tutor?"

"Yes! The tutor, yes." Max embraces the cover. Unsure what the mothers have been told, upon arrival she always follows their lead.

Mrs. Stetson flips the towel over her shoulder. "Her

friend Shannon just called to let me know you were coming, which was strange. Do you tutor many of the kids at
Stuyvesant?"

"I tutor all over the city, actually. I work by referral,
so, yeah."

"Can you see if you can get Bridge to come down
for some food? I really think she should eat something.
She skipped dinner. She's been locked in her room since
I got home. Probably on the phone with her boyfriend."
Bridget's mother holds the door open, and Max steps into
the front hall, where a day's worth of the family's bags
and shoes have been discarded.

"I brought some snacks." Max points to her bag.
Bridget's mother looks at it, the imposing red leather,
the iconic H clasp, and then to Max, her impeccable
knockoff and professional attire working to their opposite
desired effect. There is a beat of distrust as the two walk
to the staircase leading to the second floor. "It's a *huge*
test," Max offers. "A lot of kids are really freaked out
about it. Don't worry, I'm an expert." Bridget's mother
nods uncertainly. Max aims for a lighthearted shrug and
heads up.

Her attuned ears pick up the muffled sobs as her toe
lifts from the last step. Max walks quickly down the
carpeted hall, following the fuzzy thump of a bass beat
meant to obscure the keening from those who were

ignorantly devouring tacos below. Throwing her shoulders back in a way that her best friend, Zach, says reminds him of Angelina-channeling-Mary-Poppins, Max turns the doorknob, stepping inside a blast of Adele, to find Bridget Stetson in a heap. Her laptop open before her, she is staring at a hundred tiny JPEGs of a carrot-haired boy riding a skateboard. Around her lie a box's worth of wadded Kleenex, like a bed of wilted roses. Bridget looks up from the screen and is met with the flash from Max's camera.

"Bridget, Shannon sent me." Max drops her bag on the blue bedspread and opens it, exchanging the camera for a sterling flask. She swiftly pours a shot of Kombucha into the cap. "I'm Max Scott, and I want you to drink this. It'll take the edge off."

"Where is Sh-Shannon?" Bridget chokes out as she mushes her damp, blond bangs off her puffy face with the back of her sweatshirt-covered hand. "I thought she was coming with you."

"She just made the referral. Drink."

Overwhelmed, Bridget swigs the shot and hands back the top with a burning cough. Max pulls a chocolate bar from her bag, opens the wrapper, and hands it off to Bridget.

"N-no. I can't even think about—"

"Eat." Max appraises the collage-covered walls and,

leaning over Bridget's desk, unlocks the window. Cool
air rushes into the room, clearing the salty scent of tissues
and tears.

"I c-can't—my st-stomach—I may n-never eat again.
I don't understand. How do you know Shannon?"
Bridget peers around Max to the closed door as if her
friend might appear. "I was just talking to her after . . .
after—" But Max knows she can't bring herself to finish
the sentence, to say "he dumped me." Not yet.

"One bar." Max places both hands on her hips.

Bridget raises an eyebrow, but does as told. Max has
never been met by resistance on an Hour One house call.
Girls are too desperate for relief to put up a fight.

"You'll see Shannon tomorrow. Right now you just
need to focus on what I'm telling you." Max watches
Bridget bite into the dark chocolate intended to fill her
dry mouth with sweetness. Bridget chews with hollow
eyes as Max sweeps the room, stealthily dropping framed
photos of the couple into her bag along with the obvious
"Taylor and Bridget" mementos. She picks up Bridget's
cell and reprograms Taylor's number to direct dial
Max's cell. She unplugs Bridget's laptop and—

"Hey!" Bridget coughs, crumbs spurting from her
mouth. "What the hell?"

"It's not safe staying here tonight. No contact with
the outside world." Max slides the machine into her

bag and withdraws a bottle of water just as Bridget finishes off the last bit. Max takes the wrapper and hands
off the bottle. She then pulls a Limoges box from her
bag. "Valerian. All natural megadose." Bridget takes the
pill and slugs it down with a sip from the bottle. "Okay."
Max picks up Bridget by her elbows and gently steers her
along the carpet. "Into bed."

Max can tell the pill is taking effect, dulling Bridget
from the shock of the stimulants and, Max hopes, flatlin-
ing her from a high that skirts the prior excruciating low.
Helping her to lie down, Max puts a hand maternally on
Bridget's forehead. Bridget mumbles something.

"Yes?" Max encourages.

"It feels like . . . like . . ."

Max turns out the lamp. "It feels like everything they
say. . . . Like he reached into your ribs and ripped your
heart out with his bare hands. Like a giant boulder has
been dropped there in its place. I know."

"It, it physically hurts." Bridget sounds surprised as she
rubs the skin just to the left of the zipper on her sweatshirt. "It feels worse than a boulder. It's like, like . . .
there's an . . . *elephant* standing on my chest."

Max nods acknowledgment as Bridget turns on her
side, tucking into a ball as tears trace the vine pattern on
her pillowcase. "My head is getting thick," she murmurs,
and Max prays that Taylor's flaying words are also getting

harder to rerun. Max lowers the volume on the iPod dock until it's off. The lulling sounds of traffic return to the darkened room.

Max stays with Bridget until her breathing is slow and rhythmic, until she is asleep. Max knows it's what the body wants in moments of such devastation, to shut down and recharge the adrenals. The tiny hit of fermentation, the magnesium in the chocolate, the homeopathic tranquilizer are just enough to signal permission to the brain to step back from what is far too painful to make sense of just now, in the immediate aftermath of impact.

Max stands, covers Bridget with the blanket, relatches the window, and secures a red card on a red cord over Bridget's wrist. CALL IMMEDIATELY UPON WAKING. Max flips the card right side up. EX, INC.

CHAPTER 2

A twenty-minute subway ride from the Stetsons finds Max returning to her bedroom office in Brooklyn, ready to wrap up the day. Stepping down under the stone stoop to what was once, a hundred years ago, the servants' entrance, Max spots a tin of cookies left for her by a grateful client who has just completed the Ex, Inc. program. Max bumps the door shut behind her and kicks off her high heels.

Ex, Inc. headquarters are located in the garden-floor apartment of her stepfather's brownstone. After bouncing around the country for the better part of Max's life, her mother, Anne, fell for a native New York, Peter Flannery, who she met while writing an article for her most recent gig with the *New Yorker*. While Max was at boarding school crashing head-over-heels-over-head in love, Anne was getting engaged and moving into a house—two things she neglected to do at twenty-two, when she had Max.

Max's parents met in grad school. But other than an affectionate friendship, Max is the only lasting outcome of their fling. Anderson Scott lives in Tampa, and the one constant in Max's life has been summers and holidays spent camped by the condo pool with a box of novels, playing gin rummy with the leathery tenants and hearing firsthand highlights of the twentieth century.

What she lived for was when her trips to Tampa overlapped with Zachary Plimpton's visits to his grandparents. She met Zach the summer after fourth grade at the pool when he complimented her toenail polish. She complimented his in turn and they've been best friends ever since, a friendship nurtured over emails and boosted by care packages and shared MP3s.

When Max put together that her mom's new house was literally just blocks from Zach—she couldn't get to Brooklyn fast enough. Sorry, Tampa.

Peter inherited the building with the long-held intention of turning the ground-floor studio over to renters, but since they haven't even found time to unpack her mom's books or hang pictures, they certainly haven't had the energy to fix up the unit and become landlords.

With a hundred bucks of babysitting money and a lot of hours of HGTV under her belt, Max went to work on the long, open space. The front of the room she designated the "office" and the back she made her bedroom. She found a couple of banged-up desks people had put out on the street, which she dragged home and painted disco-ball silver. The chaise was a thrift-shop find she updated with more paint and a velvet throw to hide the cat-shredded upholstery. The chandelier she rescued from the Dumpster outside a gut renovation two blocks over. And the screen shielding her bed had been in Peter's bachelor pad. But the pièce de résistance is the wallpaper. Black velvet flocked on a cranberry-red background. It is high design. It is stunning. It is, in fact, wrapping paper. Lovingly and meticulously Blu-tacked to the walls one rainy weekend by Max and her staff.

"Please hold." Phoebe, Max's second assistant, mutes her headset. A sophomore at St. Mary's Academy, she has been skate-sliding the hardwood in her striped knee socks, as she is wont to do when fielding incoming calls. Phoebe loves working for Ex, Inc. because at school she feels like just one of the kilted masses, and at home, where she is one of identical triplets, she has had it with being called Claudia or Elizabeth. Ex, Inc. is her only place to be wholly herself and contribute to something she believes might be unique in all the world.

"Hi!"

"Hiya." Max hands off the cookies to Phoebe. Even though Max requests that her satisfied clients repay her only by helping out with future cases—Max never knows where one girl's family business might come in handy with another's recovery—many still insist on sending *something*. In fact, the cookies have been coming more frequently these days, and the whole floor is starting to smell like a bakery. Max pulls off her coat and heads over to the refrigerator.

"Trish Silverberg's ex joined the film club *and* is challenging her position as film club president," Phoebe says, bringing Max up to speed on her caller's predicament.

"He is? What's it been—two weeks?"

"Three since he 'just wants to be friends' at her grandmother's memorial service. Total tool." Phoebe clicks back on. "Hey, Trish, thanks for holding."

"I'm on it," Max says. "Just need to refuel." She tugs open the mini-fridge in what remains of the kitchenette. She has decoupaged it with tear sheets from fashion magazines, the door a kaleidoscope of kick-ass and fabulous.

Phoebe nods sympathetically as she listens. "Max is so

on it, Trish. And remember, he's entitled not to love you anymore." Phoebe pulls the chewed pencil from atop her head, two black braids flopping to her shoulders. "But he's not entitled to mess with your happy place."

"That's it! That's our company Christmas card." Zachary, now also known as Max's first assistant, appears in the garden doorway, working an iPhone, its protective case perfectly matching his new green contacts.

Max scrounges in the fridge. "Zach, where're the thank-you snickerdoodles?"

"I took them on my picnic date with Tom. I didn't want them to go to waste."

"I'm going to start telling clients: please, in lieu of gifts, just feed Zachary and his boyfriend."

"Don't get testy. We left you the brownies."

Max snags one and deposits her handbag on the chipped Formica counter (*that* she just has to live with). Phoebe replenishes the handbag from the kitchen cabinet, which contains, maintained at a military level of organization: bars of chocolate, bottles of Vitamin Water Zero, boxes of Kleenex Pocket Packs, packets of valerian imported from Switzerland, binoculars, telephoto lenses, Flip cams, night vision goggles, and camouflage gear. All funded, along with Zach's and Phoebe's salaries, when Ex, Inc. received a sizable donation from one of Max's early clients. Number four out of their

current alumnae roster of thirty-two. A deeply apprecia-
tive girl with deeply plunging family pockets, grateful to
be deeply over the guy who dumped her via voice mail
from his parents' private jet. Phoebe extracts the seized
laptop and hands it off to Zach.

"Bridget Stetson's laptop," Max explains.

"Thoughts on Silverberg's ex?" Zachary asks while
appraising the faded Kings of Leon stickers haphazardly
plastered across the stainless-steel top.

"Silverberg's ex," Max repeats absently as she goes to
slide the entire cookie tin from the fridge and carry it
back to her chaise.

Phoebe follows, helping herself to a brownie as she
jogs Max's memory. "The freak who's obsessed with
his own feet. The one who takes his shoes off in the
cafeteria to show how he pronates, and eats with his
hands, and is always touching everyone. Such a disgusting combo—"

"Thank you, Feebs. All of which she will totally be
seeing clearly by the time she completes the program.
She's so close to graduation, but this election thing is
no joke. A booster is definitely in order," Max reflects,
dropping down onto the stunning, if smelling slightly of
cat, chaise.

Zach sits on the front of his desk and picks up his

notebook. "Public competition can reheat hormones faster than a microwave. We don't want this going into Angie Riverdale territory." Zach invokes the name of one of Max's early cases: the one who didn't follow Max's advice and ended up getting dumped—twice. Ex, Inc. legend has it that there was no coming back from that.

"No, we don't," Max agrees. "I'll be your best friend if you go grab me some milk," she entreats.

"I already hold that honor. Phoebe?" Zach looks to her, invoking his status. Phoebe goes to get a glass for Max with a dramatic sigh.

"Thanks, man," Max says appreciatively. "My feet are killing me. I had two Hour Ones back-to-back."

"So," Zach prompts, bending forward to pick through the brownie debris. "For Trish—which booster? The 'Oh, right, he sucks'? The 'I can't be bothered'? Or the 'Screw him and the horse he rode in on'?"

Max gives it consideration until Phoebe returns with the milk. "First half: 'Screw him and the horse.' Second half: 'Can't be bothered.'"

"And how about the 'Drive it home'?"

"Ummmm, book her on the hot-air balloon ride."

"Fabulous." Zachary scribbles.

Checking the time, Phoebe throws up her hands. "*Crap!* Thursday night. Josh's chess tournament." She reaches for her backpack, not wanting to be late to cheer on her boyfriend.

"Tell him I said to rock it." Max lifts a victory fist.

"And I'm meeting you downtown for recon," Zach reminds Max, scrolling her schedule on his phone as he hops down to leave.

"Right. You'll scrub Bridget Stetson's laptop? I want this Taylor downloaded to a memory stick as tiny as his you-know-what."

"Done."

"Thanks, guys!" Max makes a prayer position with her hands, and Phoebe curtsies.

A half hour later, Max is labeling a new folder *Bridget Stetson* when her mother calls down the stairs from the family kitchen. "Max! Can you come up?"

"Sure!"

Max takes the folder and slides it under the pile of college guides she keeps prominently on her desk in case her mother does wander down. After several rounds of screaming matches that made passing dogs cower, Anne let Max drop out of St. Something's on the condition that she got her GED, aced the SATs, and applied to nine colleges. Max is hoping that just meeting the first two conditions will suffice.

Last winter Max walked out of the Met the day of her

epiphany with a clear sense that whatever was next for her academically had to be about her mission. Her mission turned into Ex, Inc., a business that was built from the ground up, relying on referrals from one friend to the next. Max needs to saturate a community to effect change, and she's not about to move away just as her work is gaining momentum.

The answer came to her at the nail salon while reading an interview with Mary-Kate and Ashley Olsen about their fashion label's new fall line. They credited their program at NYU with giving them the freedom to grow their business while they got their education. Bingo! She could keep her local client base—and design her program around the thing she was most passionate about. Even better, when her mother got itchy to move on like she always does, Max would have roots of her own already established. Nothing would jeopardize her work. Of course she hasn't told her mother about Ex, Inc. yet. Or that she's only applying to NYU. She's waiting until she has the letter of acceptance in hand.

"You rang?" Max inquires as she climbs the carpeted stairs to the parlor floor, where her mother is slicing into a ball of mozzarella in the kitchen. "You're having cheese for dinner again? Where's Peter?"

"He's working late, and it's all I can stand to eat," Anne says, turning sideways so Max can appreciate the full girth of her seven-month baby bump.

"Let me make you some pasta," Max offers.

"No, I have to go back into the office. I came home to wait for the crib to be delivered—but the guy's late. Can you handle it?"

"Sure—he's just dropping off a crib?"

"And putting it together. If we waited for Peter and me to have a free moment, this baby would sleep in a drawer." Anne wraps up the cheese and dunks it back in the fridge. The upside of having two workaholic parents is that no one notices Max is building a burgeoning business in the basement; the downside is that no one notices Max. "How're the applications coming?" Anne asks as she grabs her keys.

"I have an opening sentence." Actually she totally finished her essay a few days after NYU released this year's topics.

"Fantastic—can't wait to read it." Gathering up her battered leather tote, Anne kisses Max good night. "Don't wait up. I love you."

"You too." Max watches her mother waddle herself out the front door. Yes, at seventeen, Max Scott is going to be a big sister. To someone who is going to get to grow up with married parents who own joint property and live in the same time zone. If Max is feeling jealous or resentful, she hasn't brought any of this up to her mother, a woman, Max long ago learned, more at home talking about homework than feelings.

Max heads back downstairs, sensing the urge to pity herself. Resisting that urge is essentially what she helps her clients do every day. Surely she can apply a little of that magic to herself.

CHAPTER 3

An hour later finds Max in the bath, carefully sliding another slice of pizza from the box resting on a nearby chair. She takes a bite and sits back beneath the Charles Schultz poster of Lucy in her makeshift psychiatric booth. A self-congratulation gift for getting her GED that she snagged at a neighborhood flea market last summer while Zach was perusing vintage pocket squares. This was minutes before snagging Phoebe, who was working the cheese-dipped-pretzel table and successfully keeping a mob of very impatient, very hungry people on the verge of heatstroke happy. Max smiles at the memory of launching into her pitch on the growth opportunity at Ex, Inc., and how Phoebe cut her off to say that as long as the gig did not involve melting or dipping, Max had her at hello.

"The doctor is *in*," Max says, reciting the sign on Lucy's booth, forcing herself to stop procrastinating.

Okay, Bridget. Bridget, Bridget, Bridget . . . She rests her neck on the cool porcelain rim, closes her eyes, and chews . . . hoping Bridget is sleeping dreamlessly. In the stillness, Bridget's pain makes Max's own chest constrict, conjuring the ghost imprint of her own elephantine heartbreak. Max redirects her mind to speculate what this redheaded Taylor is doing right about now . . . fist-bumping some dude . . . sports drinks in their hands . . . carefree grins on their faces—

The buzzer rings and the water sloshes as Max sits forward, crust clenched in her teeth.

She leaps up, drops it in the box, throws on her big terry cloth robe, and wraps her long, brown hair in a towel. "Coming!" she cries as the buzzer rings again. She unlocks the door and sticks her head up under the stoop. "Hello?"

A tall, dark-haired guy in a navy-blue jumpsuit appears. Not at all what she expected. "Cooper Baby," he says gamely.

"I'm sorry?"

"Delivery from Cooper Baby. You ordered a crib?"

"Yes." Realizing in the oversized robe she could be a *Teen Mom* episode, Max gestures to the stoop above her. "Um, *I* didn't. My mother did. Can you carry it? The nursery's on the second floor."

"No problem." He retreats to the sidewalk, where the large carton is strapped to a handcart.

"Hold on—let me lock this door and run up and let you in."

Seventeen-year-old Ben Cooper huffs the handcart up the steps, trying to make it appear easy and effortless. Usually he doesn't care what it looks like when he makes his dad's deliveries, but usually he is trailing a very pregnant woman, perhaps he himself is trailed by a toddler or two. But that is the extent of who observes his after-school job. Not once has anyone close to his age factored into his rounds. For the first time he finds himself wishing he hadn't worn the jumpsuit.

As Max waits for him to bump the box up the stairs, she should be wishing she hadn't grabbed her mother's old robe, but instead is so distracted by the texts coming in from Zach as he scrubs Bridget's laptop, that she is unaware of the boy-ness of this boy. Right now he is just representing yet another odd and uncomfortable thing she has to do for her mother's new life.

"So where do you want it?" Ben asks as he wheels the box along the second-floor landing past her mom and Peter's bathroom.

"The yellow room." She points.

"With the teddy bear border? Yeah, I figured. I meant in the space."

"Oh. Um, do I have to decide?" Max asks as she flips on the overhead light.

"No. It's easy to slide around once it's assembled." He lowers it to the yellow carpet, slips a box cutter from his back pocket, and starts slicing the packaging apart. Max hops up on the dresser and tips off her turban, her wet hair flopping down her back.

Ben is suddenly nervous. Which is stupid because he could put a crib together in his sleep. Which is a skill he will do *what* with in life, he has no clue. If his dad has his way, Ben'll come back from college and be the third generation to run Cooper Baby. But Ben has to believe his life is going to be more than keeping up with the latest-model diaper pail.

"Do you know what you're doing?" Max asks as the thing he's building in front of her is starting to look more like a small cage than a sleep spot.

"Um, I—uh—never assembled this brand before. It's

new. I was kind of following what I've done before with other models."

"So you're having your learning curve—right here, right now?" She makes it sound dirty.

Blushing, he nods.

"Hang on." She runs all the way downstairs to swipe a T-shirt and pair of black jeans off the floor. Dressed for crib battle, she runs back up, pulling her hair into a damp topknot. She has no idea how beautiful she is.

"Okay," she says. "Take that child-sized torture chamber apart, pass me the directions, and let's start from scratch, assuming nothing. Lay those big pieces flat across from each other—I think they're the legs." She peers at the instructions. "So, how long have you been doing this?"

"Deliveries? Since I could walk."

"For babies, from babies—I like it. Good business model. I think maybe start with those two pieces." She hands him back the directions.

"Ah, thanks. It's my family store. You got a family store?" he asks, attaching the frame base with a Phillips head she passes him.

"I don't even got a family," she cracks. "And I want to do my own thing—no offense."

"No, me too," he says, tightening a screw. "I'd totally move to—whatever is on the opposite side of the planet." *If I could,* he thinks.

"That might be water. I would definitely double-check that before you write your admissions essay."

He smiles. She probably has a boyfriend with a cool after-school job. Like a club promoter's assistant. Or stockbroker.

"Max," she says, holding up her palm.

"Ben." He points with embarrassment to the oval name tag sewn to the front of his jumpsuit.

"That's kind of retro and awesome," she says. "I think Marc Jacobs is doing name tags next season."

"And then hairnets?"

"Inevitably." She looks back down at the directions on the carpet.

"And I'm taking any and all advice on the college essay front, so . . ." He pulls his attention away from her face and back to the friggin' crib.

"Write about whatever you're most passionate about."

"That's it?"

"Yes," Max affirms as she hands him the last screw.

"Had not heard that, thank you."

"Generic, but true." Max shrugs as a slew of texts comes into her BlackBerry.

"Okay, tah-dah!" he says, hiding his left hand and the small gouge that's starting to bleed. She looks up from her clients' daily questions of desperation along the lines of "Can't I just text him?" Most of which require only a

"NO! XO, M" response.

"Tah-dah?" she asks.

"Pregnant moms like a 'tah-dah.' It's my dad's brand of customer service."

"Well, I'll try it on my mom when she gets home."

Ben starts packing up the discarded wrapping.

"Wait!" Max runs out of the room and across the landing and comes lumbering back with a stone statue of Peter's.

Ben's eyes widen. "What're you—" She lobs it over the crib railing. The mattress bounces—and holds.

"Okay," she says, nodding appreciatively. "Well done. You're good to go."

"Need anything else?" Ben finds himself asking, not wanting to go back to his van and his homework and his dad's TV droning on into the night as one *Law & Order* episode bleeds into the next.

Max glances around. "Just a baby."

"Well, here's our fridge magnet." They lock eyes for a brief moment as she takes the pacifier-shaped logo from his warm fingers. "We have everything you want."

A few hours later, Max finds herself replaying Ben's offer as she looks out at the bustling floor of the bowling alley. Zach trails her, taking notes in preparation for a client's culmination of the Ex, Inc. program, what

Max and her team have come to call "The Moment," a carefully orchestrated event that takes place at the end of the four weeks of each client's recovery. In addition to focusing on healing, Max and her staff put each girl through rigorous training so she can finally face her ex from a position of confidence—a "Moment" to prove to herself and the guy who dumped her that she's over him.

Tonight the place is packed with NYU students, enjoying some ironically vintage entertainment, souped up with a DJ and martinis. Max can't wait to be one of them next year. "The light in here is really—off," Max observes. "It has, like, an orange cast to it. Make a note for Kelly's makeup. I'm not sending her in for her Moment looking like she passed out in a tanning bed. And you got the floor map with the emergency exits?"

"Check. And check." Zach makes a flourish with his pen as he follows behind Max. The two casually weave among the clusters of rowdy bowlers as if ambling to meet up with friends.

"How're Kelly's skills coming along?" Max inquires.

"Good. She's been taking the bus out to Jersey every Saturday to practice unobserved. She's going to bowl his pants off."

"I wonder if she should have a special, colored ball." Max pivots to him and slurps from her soda straw. "Should she have a special ball? Pink or red or something? Or is that too 'I will now break into my musical number'?"

Zach flops his dark hair from side to side, considering this detail. Around them people cheer as the thunderous sound of falling pins breaks over the whir of spinning balls. "I do love a colored ball. . . ."

"Over the top," Max deems, poking her straw into the ice chips. "Add five minutes to the schedule for her to pick out a ball from here before she goes into makeup."

Zach scribbles this down while Max bites the straw and narrows her eyes at Kelly's ex, Rufus, and his lame boyz. Bowling and checking out the hotties. Completely unaware that at this very moment Kelly is doing her kickboxing, beefing up her bowling muscles, preparing to show him no mercy.

"Eyebrow." Zach reminds Max not to make a stink face as he drops his notebook into his messenger bag.

Max relaxes her expression, tossing her plastic tumbler into the trash as they swing past. "Thanks."

"And we out." Zach leads the way to the elevator through the arriving crowds. He wedges in and sticks out his hand for Max. She takes it and squeezes beside him. Even though he's a year younger, Zach is one of the tallest Packard juniors. He has a full six inches on her, so Max must peer up to telegraph her thoughts to him as the doors seal them in with way too much olfactory information.

"Axe. Is. The. Devil," he mouths. She starts to crack up just as they are spit out onto the evening bustle of University Place.

She takes a deep inhale of the first really cold night of the season to clear her prickled sinuses. "I'm launching my own campaign that says spraying that stinky crap all over your sorry ass will get you the opposite of kissed. Cleanliness. Cleanliness will get you kissed. And cuteness. Cuteness will help—"

"And disco!" Zach begins to swing his hips to the music blasting from the speakers beneath Bowlmor's awning.

"No, not—"

"Yes! It's time." Zach throws a finger into the air. "Do it, Max. You know I won't stop." He dances in front of her, starting to draw the attention of those in line for the elevator to the bowling alley.

"Zachary."

"We are dancing!"

She lifts her pointer finger and mirrors his movement.

"Up, there she goes! But I need a hundred percent!"

She throws herself into it, making every guy waiting for the elevator suddenly wish he was staying right here for the evening, until Zach promptly stops, lifting his hair off his face. "Was that so hard?"

"Yes." She catches her breath, suppressing a grin as he

waves down a cab. "Seriously, Zach, your dance attacks are going to get us into trouble."

"The target is two floors above us with his head up a bowling ball. Oh, and about Taylor."

"Yeah, what did you find?"

"He was with Bridget four months and six days, based on her email log, and they've known each other since, like, the womb. He laid it on thick, this one. I looked through the last few weeks of his emails for warning signs, but, I mean, if I was her sassy best friend, I'd have been sewing her prom dress."

"Oy."

"And there's a kicker."

"Hit me."

"She lives *directly* across the street from him. Bedroom stares right into his."

"Wow." She pauses to take in the enormity. "New challenge. Okay, kick ass on calc tomorrow! Bye!" She kisses Zach on the cheek before walking away toward the subway.

Max sighs contentedly as she makes her way to Union Square, her tasks for the night completed. She relishes the feeling of being worn out by a full day of work, looks forward to getting into bed and waking up fresh tomorrow to tackle this new challenge of getting Bridget over the boy-next-door. Which is way worse than boy-from-camp, boy-in-school-play, or even boy-in-homeroom. She's learned that there's bound to be a strategy, she just has to think long and hard and shake down what the world doesn't even know it has to offer.

Nothing makes Max happier than the emails from her graduated clients reporting on *their* happiness. She makes a point of staying up on everyone's progress, all the way back to Client One, Olivia Petra. A few days after Max's Met epiphany, Max spotted her sobbing on a barrel of sardines behind her family's Italian grocery. Max approached her, laid out her mission, and asked if Olivia would be open to being her guinea pig. Olivia said anything was worth a shot as she couldn't feel worse than she did. Through trial and error (which Olivia thankfully had a sense of humor about—Max will never again take anyone to the totally depressing Tibet Center to work on focus), Max honed her program. At the end of four weeks, Olivia walked into senior homeroom and didn't even blink as she watched her ex suck her cousin's face. Olivia was so grateful she referred a friend, and slowly the word spread.

As she passes through the northern tip of NYU's campus, she gets excited anew about her plans. A self-described optimistic realist, Max knows colleges aren't exactly falling over themselves to admit high school dropouts. Even ones with a 3.8 GPA. So she knows she has to bring something amazing to distinguish herself. After some measured cyber-stalking (how many fan letters do psych professors get?), just this week Max was completely floored to hear back from NYU's Professor Jane Schmidt. The renowned psychologist hailed for her groundbreaking work in pain management. She is intrigued by Max's work and has agreed to meet in December to review Max's findings on "Strategies for Ameliorating Heartbreak in the American Adolescent Female." If Max's presentation is stellar and her data sound, Jane will vouch for Max to the admissions committee.

Then Max can co-major in psychology and business so she can take Ex, Inc. national. A branch in every mall. An article in every magazine. Max will be the one in the history books—the famous woman who cracked heartbreak.

Sure, equal pay, maternity leaves, and pro sports are important. But a girl can't make a free throw from the foul line if her head's not in the game. *This* is the next frontier.

CHAPTER 4

Taylor Bradley wakes the next morning with a start, the tense anticipation that's bummed him out the last few days still gripping him before he remembers . . . he did it. He broke up with Bridget. It's done—behind him! He feels a rush as he drops his feet to the floor and ruffles his hair. His *single* hair. That some girl could rub at anytime. Any girl. Because he can do that now, 'cause he's single. He scrolls his iPod in search of the perfect anthem to start this new era of his life. Settling on Drake, he rolls the volume up and raises a fist pump in his dresser mirror. What to wear his first day back?

What are guys even wearing now? He feels at the scruff on his chin as he dances into the hall and to the bathroom to shower. He should totally get a haircut, let the world know what's up. And sayonara to that scruff Bridget thought was sexy. Time for other chicks who find a shaved guy hot, 'cause he can meet them now. *Razor, please! Don't mind if I do.*

Then he's all fresh and clean. *A clean slate,* he thinks, as he pulls on his oxford and loops his school tie around his collar. He'd had a thing for Bridget since her family moved in across the street in kindergarten. She was always so cute with her blond curls, always cracking herself up. And then—when they finally got together—man. But it's his *senior year.* He can't go to college committed to the same girl he's always liked! What if they got married? He'd have been with one girl his *whole life.* When Carrie hit on him homecoming weekend, he totally clammed up. It was like he was already married. And that's when he knew what he had to do.

This summer he and Bridget hung out so much his friends started calling them by one name, "Baylor." He sends out a mass text with a triumphant grin on the way downstairs. "Baylor RIP." He hops the last two steps and slip-slides into the kitchen, where his mother is flipping through the paper at the counter. She tucks her blouse into her skirt with one hand.

"Morning, Tay." She takes a long sip of coffee without looking up, like it's any other day and not the first of the rest of his life.

"You want toast?" his dad asks from where he rummages in the fridge, holding his tie to his chest. "Anyone? Going once . . ."

"I don't know, Dad," Taylor announces as he slaps both hands down, billowing the *Journal*. "I don't know because every morning, Bridge brought me a Pop-Tart. Strawberry with sprinkles, and the thing is—I was so sick of it. Day in, day out. Strawberry and sprinkles, strawberry and sprinkles, strawberry and sprinkles. I stopped thinking about what *I* wanted for breakfast. I stopped thinking about what I *want*. I may want toast. I may want an egg. I may want lasagna! It's time I figure that out, figure *me* out. I get to meet myself for the first time in—"

"Four months?" Taylor's eight-year-old sister, Daisy, asks through a mouthful of Honey Nut Cheerios.

"And a week," Taylor corrects her.

"So, no to toast?" His dad tucks the bag tag in his teeth as he withdraws a slice of bread.

His mother shakes her head in dismay. "Does Mrs. Stetson know about this?"

Taylor's phone buzzes, and he looks down to see his best friend's response. Finally, something worthy of the occasion! "Dude. You have been sorely missed."

* * *

Outfitted in a pair of riding pants and a cozy cashmere sweater from her Etsy knitting hookup, which allows her to radiate the comfort necessary on Day One, Max slips inside Bridget's bedroom. Having received Bridget's dazed call at dawn, Max has already breezed past Mrs. Stetson with a handoff of a dozen homemade cranberry muffins and a mention of "last-minute flash-card drills." After a quick appraisal of Bridget, Max reaches into her red bag, pulls out a stainless-steel thermos, and sets it on the nightstand. She glances out at the windows across the street. Taylor's are dark, and light is filtering through the shutters on the first floor. Which means either he's already downstairs or Max has beaten his alarm clock and can preemptively close Bridget's curtains before her client awakens and does anything she'll regret. Max flicks on the bedside lamp.

"Morning, Bridget."

"All those nights we'd talk for hours, watching and waving through our windows. Teasing him with flashes of my new bra," Bridget murmurs into her pillow as if they were mid-conversation. "Maybe I misunderstood. Maybe he meant something else. It just doesn't make sense that he could go from remembering that I loved peanut-butter ice cream on Tuesday to needing to take a break on Wednesday. . . ." As Bridget's eyes focus on Max, Max lifts Bridget's head as if she were a wounded soldier and puts the thermos lid of espresso to her lips, but Bridget keeps talking. "I want to go back to sleep so I can wake up and have it be that this didn't really happen. That he didn't really dump me."

"But he did. Drink," Max encourages her. Bridget sips.

"Rule number one: caffeine is your new best friend. Liquid optimism."

"I just . . . it hurts. So. Much."

"Mornings and evenings are the worst," Max says as she pulls her up to sitting to give her the Day One speech. "But every day there's going to be a little window of time where you feel not just 'barely alive,' not just 'okay,' but positively euphoric. Winning *American Idol* euphoric. And that window is going to get longer and longer each and every day. Because your body knows that surviving this . . . elephant is going to bring you a level of strength you have not yet known. I promise. And my system will speed what organically can take months, or years, to a few weeks. Today we're aiming for about a thirty-second window, okay?"

Bridget drops her head to Max's shoulder.

"Fifteen?"

Bridget nods.

"Okay, now let's start with a shower. You'll feel better."

"But after the shower is dressed, after dressed is break-fast, after breakfast is leaving. When Taylor won't be waiting downstairs for his morning kiss and Pop-Tart before we split up for school. Because we split up for *real*." Bridget buries her face in her raised knees, the idea of taking a single step unbearable. "I won't feel better."

Max pats her sweaty back. "But I will." She stands and claps her hands. "Okay! You have homeroom at eight twenty, and we have a ton of ground to cover. Being late today of all days is not cool—in fact, for the next month I don't care if you get wombat flu, you *will* be at school every day looking awesome because that *will* get back to him and that will be the first chink in his ego. Okay, time to wash off the last twelve hours! Here we go! The rest of your spectacular life awaits!"

Bridget stares at Max, salty tear-crusts in the cor-ners of her eyes and mouth. "Sorry. So you're Shannon's friend? I'm just not really following how you—"

"We'll get to that. Take the coffee in with you. Right in under the water. Here." She pulls Bridget to her feet, hands her the lid, and holds the edge of the floral com-forter. It trails off Bridget's shoulders like a queen's cape as she shuffles to the bathroom.

While Bridget showers, Max does an informed sweep of the room, removing the sweatshirt, stuffed duck, and dangly earrings Zach's electronic espionage revealed were gifts from Taylor. She then returns the hacked laptop to Bridget's desk. Lastly Max whips out her sterling tape measure, another flea market score, and sizes up the windows.

Minutes later, Bridget, in a fresh long-sleeved tee and cords, her wet hair in a bun, sits cross-legged on the carpet across from her TV, devouring a warm breakfast wrap Max brought from the deli. Max connects the TV to her own laptop, and her PowerPoint appears with the acronym CPSRW.

"This is your schedule," Max says forcefully. "Up! Out of bed! And directly downstairs to the kitchen for a sugar-free caffeinated beverage—"

"Sugar free?" Bridget asks through a mouthful of egg.

"No Coke. No Red Bull. No Frappuccinos. We can't risk you getting artificially hyped and doing something ill advised." She clicks to the next slide, a photo of one Lorena Bobbitt. "Cut off her ex's penis." Then she advances the screen to Clara Harris. "Ran over her cheating husband three times. And we're not going out like that, not because it wouldn't feel spectacular, but because we want you ending up fabulous." She advances the screen to a sunny picture of a gorgeously grinning Jennifer Aniston. "Not fettered and reduced to a Lifetime TV bio-pic. This is about the long haul,

Bridget, not immediate gratification. Immediate gratification and lawlessness make you one thing: a psycho.
That's not my program. So! Caffeine and one serving
of lean protein to keep you from getting foggy. Then
straight to the shower, followed directly by the donning
of *real clothes*—no pj's or sweats—anything you pull on
when you have the flu does not count. Also." Max pulls
an Estée Lauder Brazen Berry lip gloss from her bag and
tosses it to Bridget.

"The gold cap says glamour and sophistication. I'm
a classic, and he's a fad. It'll lift your spirits. Reapply
between every class. So, caffeine, protein, shower, real
clothes, and . . ." She pulls a bottle of Evian from her
bag. "A minimum of two liter bottles of water to be
nursed throughout the day. Little known fact: dehy-
dration and depression go hand in hand." She flashes a
rapid succession of slides. "Virginia Woolf, Sylvia Plath,
Courtney Love. Crazy? Maybe. Depressed? Probably.
Dehydrated? Definitely. It's astounding how the lack of
electrolytes can suck a girl's mojo. In conclusion, every
morning, without fail. Caffeine. Protein. Shower. Real
clothes. Water. CPSRW. I'm tacking it to the ceiling over
your bed."

Bridget's shoulders sink as she finishes off her wrap;
Max is losing her.

"You need this big."

Max surveys her surroundings before lifting a poster of Olympian Lindsey Vonn from its spot. She pulls the cable from the television and attaches a device to the laptop, which shifts its projection, now life-sized, to the cleared wall. There is a picture of Bridget some time last spring, laughing with friends while the sun sets behind her shoulder. An arrow appears over one of the girls.

Bridget drops her head to the side, her voice wistful. "Shannon."

"Shannon has provided my services to you. Just as one of her friends provided my services for her."

"With Todd," Bridget says, putting it together. "She got over him *so* fast."

"Precisely." Max beams.

"But why didn't she tell me she worked, or whatever, with you?"

"I do not involve peripherals; I rely solely on past clients when at all possible. This is a program I designed when I discovered that girls who have been forcibly benched need way more than society has to offer to get back in the game. My associates and I will work with you over the next month as you go from this—" She clicks to a photo of a bald, post-divorce Britney taking an umbrella to a paparazzo's car window. "To this." The slide flips. "There she is, radiant and triumphant, headlining the number-one tour of the year." She turns from the projection. "Have you ever kickboxed? Total rush." She advances the screen to a photo of a glistening J. Lo. "We will not finish until Taylor fully comprehends the magnitude of what he has thrown away, until he is left with a last image of you as pure perfection in his mind."

Bridget's watery eyes light up over her red nose. "I'm in."

"Welcome aboard. Okay, so a few logistical details. This morning I am walking you to the bus stop. From now on one of my assistants, Phoebe or Zachary, will meet you on your stoop to make sure you head left, stay left, and don't even look right. Thank God you guys go to school on opposite sides of the city. This living-across-the-street thing is—sheesh."

"I've known him since we were five."

"Hm?" Max tilts herself down to hear her better.

"We played Power Rangers together. We used his mom's shoes as beds for our Giga Pets. And then last year we both studied *Our Town*. We were gonna be like George and Emily. When he kissed me, he said it was like it was always meant to be. What did I do wrong? Why did he change his mind?"

Max gently takes Bridget's chin and tilts her face up. "Guys say a lot of things. And that is right where we will pick up tomorrow after school. You have one job until then: NO CONTACT. You will stay away from that window. There are no answers out there. If I find out— and I will—that you've gone near that window, I will paint it black. Are we clear?"

Bridget twists her lips at the mandate. "Yes."

"Good. Now, finally, Bridget, no matter what impulsive crazy overtakes you in the interim, get a tattoo, pierce something private, go goth, but do not, do not, do not cut your hair." She flashes to a Photoshopped slide of how Bridget would look shorn like Victoria Beckham. "This will not make anyone regret anything."

That night Max's client Kelly sublimely bowls her program to completion and her ex, Rufus, into second-guessing himself. Kelly's Moment went off without a hitch. By design The Moment showcases a client's new-found mastery of something her previous disdain for or fear of, or just plain apathy toward, was one of her ex's pathetic reasons why they just weren't right for each other. A client's stellar display and "whatever" attitude effectively destabilize her ex's sense of certainty about his verdicts.

Rufus will no doubt be texting Kelly within the next twenty-four hours. And, as with all of Max's graduates, Kelly will no longer care, finally understanding that assessing her entire self-worth based on how this one kid sees her is flat-out crazy. The Moment totally flips the script every time, and Max loves it.

As the cab turns away from Bowlmor, a triumphant Max looks eagerly out the window at the campus she hopes—no, she *needs*—to be next year. The car slows to a red light at the top of Washington Square Park, where a couple is making out by the fountain. Max notices that the girl has impeccably barrel-curled hair, the kind that takes the better part of an hour, and is wearing very high heels. Max looks down at her own suede boo-ties, so glad she isn't trying to dress for a boy anymore. Getting Ex, Inc. off the ground has been too consuming for her to let herself be distracted by dating, especially when she bears daily witness to the aftermath.

Max's eye lingers on the guy's arm circling round the girl's waist, torquing her frame into his. Max indulges in a brief pang of nostalgia, same as when she catches a few seconds of *The Notebook* on cable, when she lets herself remember what it felt like to be kissed that hard. A trio of guys walks in front of the couple, obscuring Max's perving. One steps closer to the curb, his blazer collar upturned against the breeze. Suddenly Max feels a cold drop beneath her ribs, like her plane just lost altitude. The stoplight changes, the cab sails forward, and Max twists to see that, yes—the blond hair, the confident grin—it can't be, it *can't* be.

But it is.

After so many months of trailing and defusing and humbling other girls' exes, Max has just laid eyes on her own.

CHAPTER 5

The next morning, Max squeezes into the F train's rush-hour throngs and waits with everyone else for the doors to close. She's supremely annoyed. Supremely.

Hugo Fucking Tillman.

In the aftermath of their breakup, it'd begun to feel like she'd made him—and the entire five-month relationship—up. Like, maybe she was just going about her business trying to conjugate verbs when she was hit out of nowhere with a fully loaded dart of "rejection toxin." Or picked up a nasty "dumped" virus after forgetting to wear her flip-flops in the dormitory showers.

Another businessman pushes into the car, where there is no space.

Hugo Fucking Tillman the Billionth. She darts her hand to the inches of available railing as the train jerks into motion—uch! Ten freaking months since she's seen him! She shouldn't even care! But she wasn't *supposed* to see him, that's the point. The Tillman family considers Manhattan an upstart compared to their rarefied corner of Boston. The first—and only—time Hugo brought her home, his mother, Vivian, offered her a cup of tea from the family service and took her for a grand tour of the Tillman photo hall of their Massachusetts estate. Vivian knew the current location of every cousin and aunt, even those in cemetery plots, which, Vivian drily shared, were behind the family chapel, left of the stables. After living out of boxes her whole life, just the idea that Max might be invited to entwine with such deep roots was enough to seduce her.

It felt like the fulfillment of a promise whispered from St. Something's brochure. A glossy catalog rife with photos that looked like Ralph Lauren's latest campaign. Mossy stone walls squaring off a lush green in the center of campus. All that mahogany, and griffins carved into everything. The clusters of guys playing rugby, and the girls smiling with books on a plaid wool blanket shot at a hazy distance.

Hazy should have been her first clue.

There not being a mall should have been her second. Not even a mall equivalent. There was a tavern by the train station where parents took their kids out to dinner when they came for a visit. And there was a gas station where they filled up their tanks to drive back home. Except the Tillmans. The Tillmans were chauffeured by a man in full livery.

These St. Something's kids had been together fore-e-ver. Their ancestors had been together forever. Lido-deck-of-the-*Mayflower* forever. They summered together in Nantucket and Martha's Vineyard. The girls wore their great-grandmothers' pearl studs and flat ChapSticked smiles. And the worst part—they didn't laugh. Not really. They were all knowing glances and mocking smirks. Max quickly realized she'd have to drop her bar way below pee-your-pants potential. After a week she would have settled for a giggle, especially one that wasn't at her expense.

Okay, so looking back, maybe it was risky to wear over-the-knee cable-knit socks and the gold chain on the first day. But she was flying blind! And it was her homage to Chanel via Abercrombie! As Max beelined for the girls' room, frantically unstringing the heavy strands from her neck, she thought, *This isn't even L.L.Bean via*

Abercrombie. This *is L.L.Bean via a casket.* Max had never been anywhere that disdained flair so intensely.

Over the following week, Max toned it down. All the way. No makeup. No quirk. No funny. Unable to make friends, she was desperately lonely. And then one humid August evening, on the last night of orientation, Hugo Tillman the Billionth, of the Concord Tillmans and the perfect blond hair, knocked on her door.

As the F train inches into Manhattan, Max indulges in the memory. The warm, fizzy rush of him. He was looking for Meredith Blah's room, but stayed to chat, leaning against the door frame, his blue eyes flitting to the red patent leather boots she wore to cheer herself when alone. She stared up at him from her desk chair, the guy who was the most St. Something's of them all. He was so at home there, so effortless.

She was shocked to discover that he secretly found everyone as tedious and boring as she did. She was drawn to his struggle to figure out who he was, apart from the Tillman legacy. Not to mention how he would soon come for her with out-of-season flowers and limo trips to four-star Boston restaurants. Fascinated with her independence, he loved her boots, her wit, her *her.* It thrilled him to hear her voice her opinions. After feeling so invisible on that campus, she was suddenly basking in a spotlight of adoration. The king bee wanted to make her his queen—what could be more validating than that?

And it all started with him leaning in her door, and her daring to remark that if *he* was lost at St. Something's, then the Earth must be off its axis. He'd actually blushed, standing there with his rugby sleeves pushed up over his tanned forearms. Is it possible to be turned on by forearms?

Oh my God. Max grips the pole as the train brakes. Oh my God! So not doing this. Screw his forearms, which will prematurely freckle and wrinkle way sooner than, than—well, the rest of us. Screw his effortless everything! Let him get on the first bus back to Blahville. *This is my town,* she thinks. *Mine.*

Having gotten Bridget safely off to school, Max multi-tasks her way along Court Street with a photo of Taylor in one hand and her BlackBerry in the other. From nine to three p.m., when Zach and Phoebe are otherwise occupied, Max tackles her prep work uninterrupted. Her experience has shown that the majority of teenage breakups occur as the day wanes, predominantly from three p.m. onward—unless a guy tries to slip one in with a between-class text. There is a certain hot ring of hell reserved for such douches. But there are so many douches—so many rings—no. *Not* thinking about Hugo until Zach gets to the bottom of why he was in New York for the night.

Shaking her hair over her shoulder, she crosses the street to duck inside Stan's Party Parthenon. "Miss Max!" Stan greets her from where he's been flipping through his *Post* on a stool behind the counter.

"Hey, Stan!" Max smiles. It's impossible not to in the Party Parthenon. Stan's densely packed shelves conjure memories of planning birthdays as a kid when she would pore over packages of flower-festooned paper plates at the local party store while her mother fact-checked on her cell. Her favorite remains the *Dirty Dancing*–themed birthday she threw in sixth grade when her mom was at the *Reno Herald*. She chose white napkins with a musical-note pattern. Everyone came dressed as either Baby or Johnny, and she made a papier mâché watermelon to carry in for her grand entrance. Zach probably still has the picture she sent him from it.

She makes her way to Stan beneath the sea of piñatas dangling from the pipes snaking overhead. The figures all tilt ever so slightly due to a well-hidden fan. "Now, Miss Max, what can I do for you?"

Max hands Taylor's snapshot to Stan. He peers through his bifocals to get a "read" on it.

"Donkey," he pronounces.

"You sure?"

Stan studies the picture of Taylor sprawled cockily on his front stoop, a heavily stickered skateboard across his knees. "A real ass. Definitely." Stan leans over the counter to direct Max's attention to a donkey-as-devil piñata hovering over the recently unpacked Halloween masks. "Insincere or"—he points up to a donkey as Santa— "judgmental and withholding."

Max squishes her lips to the side with her index finger, her gaze ping-ponging between the two. "Mmm . . . the prior."

"Done. And I have something for you!" Stan pulls her previous order from under the counter—a pig in a tutu.

"Perfect." She swivels the piñata around to check that the grinning face of Jen's ex is lasered where the pig's face should be.

Not long after three p.m. that afternoon, Max holds said pig under one arm while standing over Jen, who has, after two weeks on Max's program, hit a minor stumbling block, leaving her sobbing uncontrollably on her bedroom floor while wildly gesticulating with a stained T-shirt and a vacuum cleaner attachment.

"Jen, you were doing so great. What happened?" Max

drops the piñata onto Jen's desk to grab a fresh pack of tissues from her handbag.

"I was deep cleaning my room like you said to. Just like you said, I was making room for the new. And then I went to vacuum the floor of my closet and remembered that he broke this—" She holds out the attachment. "When he tried to suck up spilled cereal. It was soggy. I never told my mom. So I went to get the dustpan, and that's where I found this." She holds up her thumb with a Chiquita banana sticker. "They're everywhere." She fans her fingers, revealing stickers on each tip. "Every time he ate a banana. He never threw them out. So, I wanted to clean them off and found this—" She holds out a shoe polish–stained cloth. "In the rag bin."

"A Minnie Mouse T-shirt. Okay . . ."

"I've had it since I was seven. He must've used it to polish his shoes when he came over before the forensics tournament."

"And . . ."

"So!" Jen is desperate to make her point. "So he was trying to help me with my chores. He was trying to dress better. He was *trying*. If only I'd given him more credit, any credit. I should have baked him cupcakes or, or I don't know, given him a hand job before he competed. I didn't make it an occasion. I should have made it an occasion! Why didn't I make it an occasion?! *Why?!*"

Max grabs her by her shoulders. "Did *he* make it an occasion when you cooked snacks every time his friends crashed your dates, wore a new outfit every time you saw him, did his physics homework? And yes, gave him a hand job? Was there a grand marshal parade for that?" Max wrests the tee and the attachment and unpeels each sticker from Jen's fingertips. "Cold shower! Let's go! While you're in there, meditate on this: soggy cereal with the vacuum? Really, Jen? *Really?*" Max pushes a Chiquita sticker onto the center of Jen's forehead and, with a quick look to make sure the route is clear of siblings, turns her to the hallway.

Waiting to hear the water running in the bathroom, Max commences searching for and scraping off Chiquita stickers with one deft move of a razor. Jen was right—they're everywhere: stuck to book covers, picture frames, electronics. Max dials Phoebe, gripping the phone with her shoulder as she climbs on Jen's desk to hang the piñata from the ceiling fan.

"Phoebe here."

"Hiya. Can you meet me at Jen's in twenty with an extra razor and a bottle of Goo Gone?"

"Can *you* fill me in on Hugo Tillman?" Phoebe retorts.

Max feels a cold heat pass through her and darts a steadying hand to the ceiling. "Phoebe."

"I'm serious. Since when do I not get clearance on a case? It sucks balls."

"Charming."

"Come on, who did this blond hottie dump? I Googled him, but all I got was a pic of him on some red carpet in *New York* magazine."

"*He's in* New York *magazine?!*" Max screeches.

"Just tell me. I get it's someone big. A debutante? Celebrity? The mayor's daughter?"

"Me," Max says simply, the floor a million miles away. "He dumped me."

Stunned silence. She can just see Phoebe's bottom jaw hanging wide, the purple rubber bands of her lingual braces stretched to their limit. *New York* magazine? Why?!

"AAAAAAHHHHHHHHHHHH!" Jen screams from the bathroom.

"I have to go. This conversation is permanently over. Eighteen minutes, Phoebe. Razor and Goo, got it?"

"Sorry, yes, got it."

The bedroom door swings open and Jen flies in, water droplets spraying the rug. Max tugs the billy club from her bag, and spins Jen toward the dangling face of her ex.

That evening Max knows what she needs. Her drug of choice, if you will. So a pinkie-nail-sized picture of

Hugo's head at some stupid party made a magazine's social roundup. What Max has going for her is so much cooler.

Her mom is working late—again. But Max doesn't mind. After meeting Anne for a burger around the corner from 4 Times Square, her gleaming high-rise office building, Max escorts her mom back to her desk, showing the appropriate filial concern for her disgustingly pregnant state. But really this gives Max the advantage of gliding past lobby security without arousing attention. Once Max has kissed her mom good-bye at the *New Yorker* offices on twenty, she gets back in the elevator and heads up two floors—on her way to her happy place, the flagship of *Teen Vogue*.

The first time she came to have dinner at Condé Nast with her mom, looked up at the elevator directory, and saw *Teen Vogue* listed, she almost fainted. So much glamour, so much potential, just two floors above Anne's army of the cerebral unadorned. Anne always has so many articles swimming behind her eyes, she would forget to change clothes if Max didn't remind her to hang today's suit at the back of her closet and pull from the front tomorrow.

That first night, Max waited until her mother was lost in work before putting down her practice AP and

casually saying she was going to get a soda. Max's
palms were sweaty before the elevator doors even
opened, revealing a wall-sized replica of that month's
cover and—even better—no glass barriers, no key card
required for access. While the building is usually empty
late at night, Max pulled herself up a little straighter
and flipped her hair just in case she had to pass someone. She tried to carry herself like an intern and walked
briskly, as if she knew where she was going, as if she
belonged.

Max told herself, as she moved hungrily along the
charcoal carpeting among the slick white cubicles, fin-
gering fabric swatches and look books, that she just
wanted to see where this vision came together. But she
knew there was one siren song calling her.

The closet.

She spotted it at the end of the hallway. Its gleaming double doors beckoning. She promised herself she'd
just peek. But as she pressed the silver handle and the
smell of fresh cloth—the scent of department stores,
of transformation and hope—hit her, she knew she
was lost. *Closet* was an epic understatement of a noun.
This was a huge room filled with racks of brand-new
clothes. So new they had never been worn by anyone;
so new, the idea of these clothes—the colors, the cuts,

the style—didn't even exist yet—just for those few
people who had made them and anyone who had been
behind this door. The care, thought, and debate that
had gone into every single stitch was just so inspiring.
And the endless possibility for self-invention that surrounded her took her breath away. Before she knew
what she was doing, she had dropped her romper to
the floor and was wearing an LF dress with a Vivienne
Tam chunky sweater. She was in heaven.

Careful to leave the racks of clothes yet to be pho-
tographed untouched, she pilfered freely from the one
labeled TO BE RETURNED. What would it matter if Vince
didn't get this cashmere wrap dress back this week?
He could wait. Rogan could live without this T-shirt.
Max turned the closet into her own personal couture lend-
ing library, always returning the items within seven days
and always immaculate.

Tonight as Max fingers the garments, planning next
week's wardrobe, she thinks about her current roster of
clients and their programs. She grabs a puffed-sleeved
Lululemon jacket in a kind of funky scuba-suit material
for boxing with Bridget, a Marni faux-fur vest for taking
Jen out to Coney Island to ride the roller coasters, and a
Burberry trench for tailing Trish Silverberg's ex to make
sure he's playing this election straight.

Then she spots it—a red silk column caught some-where between a dress and a slip, so perfectly cut that it makes Max look naked and perfectly clothed at the same time. Max spins in the mirror, taking in her reflection. Unlike the jacket or the vest or the trench, this is not armor designed to help her look like the in-control per-son her clients need her to be. This is, to put it simply, a date dress. A dream-date dress. This is the dress you wear to get the guy.

She feels her eyes water as her phone glows to life on the floor.

"Zach?" she answers. "What do we know?"

"Yeah, why don't you meet me downstairs?"

"You're here?"

"By the revolving doors."

She quickly hangs the dress back up, packs her massive tote, and hustles to the elevator bank, riding down to the first floor with her booty over her shoulder. She nods at the guard as she spins through the security turnstile to see Zach looking uncharacteristically small under the two-story granite ceiling.

"Zachary! What're you doing? You could have just given me the report over the phone." She follows him out through the revolving door onto 42nd Street.

"I wanted to be here." He unpeels his green scarf and

drapes it around her as she lowers the bag between her ankles. "Hello, Father Christmas."

"I got a Marni vest you will want to rip off my corpse. Okay, don't be so dramatic—just tell me. Hugo's here for a whole week?"

Zach presses his thin lips together.

"Spill it." She wraps her arms around herself. "You found his hotel. I'll just avoid the neighborhood. He'll get back on a plane and head off to wherever he's going to college—Harvard—he's, like, twelfth-generation Harvard—his family went there *and* built it during breaks between classes. I can deal with a few days of lying low—"

"Or months?"

"Months?"

"Years?"

"Years!"

Zach splays his fingers. "Okay. I recognized the jacket he's wearing in that picture is *this* season's John Varvatos."

"You have freakish skills."

"*Gracias.* So I called *New York* mag pretending to be from John Varvatos saying we wanted to contact him about spokesperson stuff, blah, blah, blah, and they gave me the number of his publicist—"

"Publicist?!" Max finds herself screeching for the second time in not just her life but in one day. "Hugo Tillman—Waspiest of the Wasps, the guy who not only has the same monogrammed velvet slippers as his seventy-two-year-old grandfather, he has the matching belt buckle—he has a *publicist?*"

"So I called the publicist pretending to be from *New York* mag—saying we got traffic off the pic on the site and were interested in doing a profile."

"And?"

"Well, she was running for an appointment and wanted to schedule a lunch. Can you imagine? But she did tell me one thing. The family has a new building downtown. Tillman Development's first venture in Manhattan, a superdeluxe high-rise. Hugo's learning the ropes."

Max makes a sound of loathing like something a snake might say if it could clear its throat.

"Since it's downtown, the company wants to project a younger, hipper image and will be—and I quote—*positioning* Hugo to be the new face of Tillman, Inc. Like Ivanka Trump. With testicles."

If Max opens her eyes any wider, her eyeballs will fall out of her head and roll across the street to the Gap. "So he'll be coming to the city all the time?"

Zach nods. "I can take her up on that lunch. Get the whole story."

For a second, Max is tempted. "No. Too high risk." Max's teeth start to chatter but it isn't that cold out.

"Look." Zach puts his hand on her arm. "We're going to the Plaza, chocolate milk-shaking up, and you're *finally* going to talk me through this. Seriously, it's cray-cray that I know nothing about what went down with you and this guy. I want every detail," Zach continues with forced flamboyance. "How you met, was it torrid, did he like you on top?"

Max looks at him. As much as she wants to, she can't—still can't bear laying the whole thing out for his unflinching analysis. "Thanks, but I'm totally fine."

A flicker of hurt creases Zach's face like the time he stepped on sea glass. They were chatting up hot surfers, and Max didn't find out he was bleeding until well after the guys paddled off. Zach deflates, his voice quiet. "Seriously, Max?"

"Totally. I'm not giving it another thought."

Instead she's thinking about this new information so hard, by the time her train pulls into the Bergen Street station she suspects it may be powering the entire MTA grid. Can they hack the PR firm's computer, get Hugo's schedule of events—and put Max on a bus to New Jersey for each one? Max bangs through the turnstile and drags her bag up the stairs like it's full of cats who've done something to piss her off.

While not up for rehashing Hugo with Zach—chocolate does sound right. She stops into the deli to scour the rows of Ritter Sport, thinking this is probably a six-bar level of shock. She's getting ready to pay when someone behind her asks, "Expecting a shortage?"

She whips around, prepared to deliver an icy glare to the lame-ass—"Cooper Baby," she says, relieved to see him instead, despite how badly she wants to be in a self-indulgently foul mood.

"Ben," he reminds her. "Whatcha up to?" he asks. "Having a magnesium party?"

"Huh?" she asks, spotting the empty can in his hand, the remaining five dangling from their plastic chokers.

"Sorry," Ben says, "AP bio exam tomorrow. Chocolate's high in magnesium. Why women crave it when they have their . . ." He trails off, turning the same strawberry color as the sticky corners of his mouth. He burps. "Excuse me."

"Did you just pound that?" she has to ask.

"I can*not* go to sleep tonight. I am four days behind on homework because of all the college stuff." Ben takes her chocolate from her and puts it on the counter. "All together," he tells the Korean guy.

"You sure?" Max appreciates the gallant gesture, but can't stop seeing Hugo right there, in *her* park, in the middle of *her* favorite neighborhood, her brain like an octopus tentacled around her indignation. "Thank you," she musters to Ben as she follows him out past the rainbow tiers of dyed chrysanthemums.

"You going this way?" He points toward her house, on Clinton Street, his basketball jacket falling open. She nods. "Me too." They start to walk. "Can I carry your luggage?"

"You *are* full service," she marvels.

"Don't mock. If my father passes us on his way home and sees me letting you struggle with that he'll hit me upside the head with your Ritter Sport."

"Well, thank you—again." She gladly hands off the bag, having underestimated the weight of prêt-à-porter outerwear.

"Okay, yes, I procrastinated," Ben says unprompted. "But it wasn't my fault." He pauses, flips the top off another can, and downs it in one go. "Ech." He wipes his mouth with the back of his sleeve. "My best friend is newly single and needs to take his oats on the town."

"Ah, yes," Max says. "The ceremonial oat tour." She reaches in the shopping bag and takes out the milk bar with almonds, ripping it open. "It must be so *hard* for guys in relationships—to have just *one* girlfriend *completely* devoted to taking care of all your whole-grain needs. I can see how at the first opportunity you'd just *have* to get out there and—sow." She can't keep the edge out of her voice.

He lifts his palms defensively. "Look, I'm not sowing anything. I'm just the wingman. I am the pizza procurer, the Yelp navigator, the fake-ID possessor."

They step over where an old tree has bumped up the sidewalk into a mogul. "So how come your friend can go out on school nights?" She moves the conversation to safer territory.

"Because he's a legacy at Kenyon." Ben stops and puts his hand to his chest. "*I* am a legacy at Gerber."

She laughs as the edges of her foul mood lighten, the tentacles loosening for a split second. "But when you get into a school—and c'mon, you will—you're going to have a confidence your friend will never have because you'll know you did it yourself. You didn't have to rely on your ancestors of yore."

He smiles back at her. Ben can't believe his luck—in either direction. Good: that he could run into Max again—looking all cute and dressed—her nose pink from the cold. That she's funny—and just seems to *get* everything he says. Bad: that he could be looking like shit from too-little sleep—burping red chemical aftertaste—and too hopped-up on *energy* to be funny back. Not that any of this matters—it's senior year—time for work. Not the time for pink noses—or funny.

They slow in front of Max's house, and she finds herself thinking of all the nights Hugo walked her back to her dorm. Uch! She wants to hit her head against the stoop railing like a swimmer knocking trapped chlorine loose.

"How's the crib working out?" he asks.

"Oh, awesome. I get in at least once a day. Read the paper." She lets herself laugh.

"Sorry—right—of course."

They stand there for a moment, like this is a date, which it so isn't. She doesn't even know why she's still standing there. Finally she holds her hands out for the bag, their fingers brushing again as he passes it off. "Okay, well, good luck with your exam," she says.

"Yeah, good luck with your . . . binge."

She gives a thumbs-up and jogs down the three steps, pulling out her keys. He notices how the light coming from the parlor-floor windows plays through her hair. "Max?"

"Yeah?"

"Can I text you?"

"Oh." She's surprised and, for the first time in a long

while, flustered by a boy.

"Or not."

"No, no, yeah, that would be great." She suppresses a smile as she tosses out her number.

CHAPTER 6

A few days later, Max watches as Zach painstakingly spreads the opaque, reflective film across Bridget's bedroom windows. "This is ridiculous," Bridget states as she stares at the beige-tinted image of herself, her arms folded across her tank top in protest. Pointedly ignoring her as instructed, Zach smoothes his palm along the thin coating, obscuring the remaining corner of bare glass and the last glimpse at the reddened leaves clinging to the oak outside.

"Uh, no, *this* is ridiculous." Max whips up a photo that's fluttered down to the blue carpet from the box they are packing and holds it to Bridget's innocent face.

"I have no idea how that got in there." Bridget bites a cuticle as Max meticulously folds the last item of Taylor's—his purple Kenyon hoodie—atop his other belongings.

"You have no idea how a picture of you in a bikini got in here. Really."

"Look, Max, he took it when we were at his beach house. Technically it's his, so I'm giving it back. That's what we're doing, right?" Bridget sits hard on her bed, looking miserable in a sea of misery.

"What we're doing is underscoring how ludicrously calm you are. Stamping 'Bridget Is a Class Act' in neon blinking lights across his forehead. Unsettling him with the complete absence of drama. What we're *not* doing is sending him photos of cleavage."

"Fine." Bridget takes the photo and throws it over her shoulder where it drops dejectedly to the puckered duvet. "Are you okay?"

"What?" Max is thrown by the personal inquiry. Clients are usually too (totally understandably) preoccupied to pursue anything more outwardly focused than where Max scored her shoes.

"You look stressed." Bridget gives her nails a rest as Zach hops down from the sill. "And you don't seem like a looks-stressed kind of girl, so I was just wondering."

"Oh!" Max tosses her hand in an emphatic "it's nothing" gesture because she would never in a million years cop to the fact that she got twitchy on the way here, thinking she spotted Hugo on a crowded street, and darted into a store to hide.

"It's her allergies." Zach covers for her as he sweeps his bangs to the side with a kelly-green varnished nail.

"In October?"

"Leaf mold," Max confirms without looking at Zach.

Bridget returns her focus to the box and drops her head to her chest. "At least let me pour the paint thinner over his sweater."

"No! No destroying, disfiguring, or dismantling. Paint thinner says—"

"I care," Zach finishes for her. "I'm desperate for you to notice that I care. I'm crazed to get your attention. I'm a psycho."

"And we are avoiding the P-word at all cost," Max pronounces as Zach goes to pull a roll of clear packing tape from her red bag and hands it to Max with a flourish. "It's time."

"Ugh." Bridget pounds both fists into the mattress. "I hate this!"

"Then let that motivate you"—Max passes the roll to Bridget—"to tape his ass up."

Bridget stares at the box containing the only tangible

evidence of Taylor's love that remains. "I loved pulling on his clothes," she says quietly. "Slipping his big sweatshirt over my head, you know? The weight of the fabric made me feel so small, like a music-box ballerina. I thought his scent of deodorant and fabric softener and the wind whipping past him as he skated was just for me."

"Bridget," Max urges gently. "It's time."

With a rip that satisfies Max and Zach, Bridget seals the flaps shut with obvious reluctance.

A few minutes later, with Max's red bag swung jauntily over his shoulder, Zach escorts Bridget to the multiplex where Shannon will meet her for a horror movie, simultaneously distracting Bridget from running the bikini photo to Taylor's mail slot and satiating her fantasies of slashing his belongings. Meanwhile, Max, cloaked in Peter's old ski parka, heads across the street to make contact. From the base of Taylor's stoop, Max turns to glance over to Bridget's bedroom windows on the second floor. Perfect. They look completely normal from out here, and there'll be no temptation. She'll add this window film discovery to her ever-growing log of tactical resources when she gets home.

Even though the patter of drops has slowed, Max keeps her hood on as she jogs up Taylor's front steps, box first. She leans her elbow into the bell.

* * *

Ben Cooper hears the door buzz from below. Or thinks he does. It's kind of hard to discern from the club mix pumping out of Taylor's computer speakers. Especially since Ben's head is picking up the vibrations from the vantage point of Taylor's bedroom floor, his socks resting up the wall as he tosses a mini basketball into the sagging hoop clipped to the top of the closet door. Taylor's dad brought it back from some medical conference when they were kids. They're taking it with them for their dorm room at Kenyon.

It suddenly strikes Ben that this dorm room will probably feel exactly like this. Ben's NBA posters will soon be covered by Taylor's skaters, all frozen forever in mid-rotation over their half-pipes. The thought causes Ben to tense his fingertips on the ball, his nail beds going purple.

Ben can't even pinpoint when he and Taylor made this plan for Kenyon in the first place. Ben's dad never went to college. The way Mr. Bradley talked about Kenyon, always cracking himself up, well, Ben's dad didn't talk about anything like that.

Up against the mess of his parents' divorce, it had been comforting to know that he could picture what college was going to look like, he and Taylor taking it on—but the more his dad talks about him coming back to run the store afterward, the more he feels like he knows what the rest of his *life* is going to look like.

The ball thuds to the floor, narrowly missing Ben's face. Taylor reaches a foot out to stop it from rolling away without looking up from clicking through Halloween party options. Ben is still figuring out how to break it to Taylor that he can't party on Halloween. Ben has to take the application workshop from that supposed college genius on November 1 that starts at eight in the freaking morning. A genius with no social life—holla! Mrs. Downing, their college advisor, would choke Ben with one of her paisley scarves if he didn't show after she "worked her magic" to get him in.

"Dude," Ben yells over the music. "That your door-bell?"

"What?"

"Doorbell!"

Taylor hits MUTE, and they both listen for a second.

"I'll get it," Ben says, happy for a chance to grab some air that is not scented with Taylor's sneakers. Down in the foyer, Ben pulls open the front door just in time to make out a hooded figure picking up speed as it heads toward Greenwich Avenue.

"Who is it?" Taylor calls from his room.

"Box for you. From a messenger."

"Grab the Fritos while you're down there."

Ben snags the orange bag from over the fridge and

brings both to where Taylor waits at the top of the stairs. "A messenger? You sure it isn't for my dad?"

Ben shrugs, handing it off and popping the chip bag. "Open it."

Taylor slices through the tape. Opening the flaps with evident curiosity, he lifts out the contents with a strange expression on his face. Ben recognizes Taylor's sweatshirt, along with his Volcom hoodie, and his GOD IS A DJ hat.

Taylor mutters something about "her perfume" as Ben watches his hands digging through the neat pile in search of—what?

"What is it?" Ben asks, mouth full of chips.

"My stuff. From Bridge. No note, no . . . anything."

Ben drops into Taylor's desk chair and swivels around to check out what Taylor's search has pulled up on the computer. Ben tells himself to just say it already. "So about Halloween . . ."

"What?"

"Not sure I can swing it this year." Ben wipes the yellow crumbs from his palms and watches Taylor for a reaction, but Taylor doesn't seem to have heard because he's just focused on putting everything back in the box. Taylor presses his hand over the slit. But the seal is already broken, and the flaps slowly rise back up.

* * *

Max feels her phone buzzing in her pocket as she rounds the corner onto Greenwich. "Bridge break free?" she asks.

"That girl's in the world's longest line for Gummi Bears," Zach says.

"Then what's up?"

"Leaf mold?" he asks.

"You said allergies!" Max protests. "Look, I just have a lot of cases right now. Yes, I'm a little stressed."

"Uh-huh." Zach sounds unconvinced.

"Seriously, Zachary, I'm fine."

"O-kay," he trills, the second syllable rising. "Up, gotta jet. The bloodbath is commencing, and the girls are passing on Gummis to grab seats."

"Yes—go!" She rushes, and he hangs up. *I am fine,* she thinks as she strides over to Sixth Avenue. *This* is *allergies. Just a* temporary *reaction brought on by proximity to asshole.*

That night Max is happily ensconced in her bunny pajamas and working on the presentation for Dr. Schmidt when she realizes she isn't sure of the year Dr. Schmidt published her first influential paper. So Max goes to the NYU site to load Dr. Schmidt's page, which leads to a student blog from the psych department, which leads to a freshman blog about NYU housing, which leads to a boy blog about hot girls on campus, which leads to an even tackier boy blog about the best secret hookup spots, which leads to a blog called *New at the U.* Max starts reading this kid's account of his first weeks at school, his adventures in the village, imagining herself in his shoes next fall.

She's just reaching for her mug of tea when she scrolls all the way down to the bottom of the page, where he's posted pictures from orientation.

And she sees Hugo Tillman grinning in front of the library with the other freshmen.

Oh.

My.

God.

He's not just visiting.

He going to NYU.

CHAPTER 7

Max pulls upon an age-old female strategy—yelling at herself like a steroid-pumped drill sergeant: "GET A GRIP! STOP BEING PATHETIC!" Which has the same effect that yelling at oneself always does; in addition to Max feeling her future threatened, she dually feels like total crap for feeling it. But come on, it's *massively* unfair! And as much as she tells her clients: "Focus on fair, get nowhere," Hugo Tillman could both be accepted into and afford to attend any happy place on the planet and he's going to hers. It's not fucking fair, and she'd say it to fair's face.

By the next afternoon, Max has worn holes in her tights pacing the floor.

"Yallo!" Zach's loafer appears on the third step.

"*How*, Zach? How did we miss this?" Max follows him as he walks to his desk. "It wasn't on his Twitter or Facebook? Seriously, I need you guys to talk me through this oversight."

"Okay." He stares at her evenly as he unwinds his scarf. "You first."

"Look," Max says, faltering. "Can't you just work on this like I'm a client?"

"You mean, can't I just work on this like I'm your employee?"

"No. Yes."

"And here I thought I was your best friend," Zach says, the sea-glass look returning full force.

"Okay!" Phoebe calls from the top of the stairs as if she's mid-conversation with them. "Guess who interviewed Hugo Tillman? Me!"

"You *what*?" Zach and Max spin to her as she jogs down, apple cheeked with her achievement.

"At lunch." She fills them in as she tosses her bag down. "I cold-called him saying I was from *Hounds and Yachts* magazine—"

"That's a thing?" Max interrupts.

"It sounded like a thing." Phoebe shrugs off her coat.

Zach and Max give an acknowledging head tilt.

"And he just talked to you?" Zach's incredulous.

"I used my cockney accent. The publicist hasn't released the NYU angle because they're, quote, waiting on that. The family's trying to present his image as youthful, but not young. Anyway, he's doing the five-year accelerated combined BA and MBA at Stern and living off campus. He had a long-haired dachshund named Huggins as a kid, and he's won three regattas and placed in seven."

"I should have gone to lunch with that publicist." Zach crosses his arms. "I could have penciled in stubble."

"He's going to Stern?" Max drops onto her chair. "We're going to be in the same business classes together? What next, he's moving in with my mom?"

"Living off campus." Phoebe checks her notes. "West Village loft."

"Why isn't he going to Harvard?!" Max implores the room.

"How should we know?!" Zach throws his hands up in exasperation. "You want to be a client, Max, but clients give us a *full backstory*. You're not telling us a freaking thing!"

Max looks from Phoebe's surprised expression to Zach's frustrated one and takes a deep breath. "Okay. Here goes. He was a senior. I was a junior. He loved everything about me until suddenly he didn't. We were together five months almost to the day. I was ousted by a girl so boring it boggles the mind. I left school. Moved here. Started this business. You're up to speed." She does not share how he shivered the first time their shirts were off beneath his scratchy wool blanket.

"That's all you're going to tell me?" Zach asks, forcing Max back to the present as Phoebe powers up her computer. "You left me ten voice mails last night. You were—"

"Thrown." Max swipes her flat palm definitively through the air. "I was thrown. We were missing pivotal information, which we now have," Max rushes. "I'm not about to start wandering the West Village in a nightie and mumbling to strangers about what could've been, Zach. I just need a little booster. Just like we did for Trish Silverberg when her ex tried to take over the film club! Remember, he's entitled not to love me, but he's not entitled to mess with my happy place."

"Okay, fair enough," Zach says as he turns on his computer.

"So where are we with everyone?" As they commence their updates, Max's eyes drift to her photo of Cate Blanchett as Queen Elizabeth. She thinks there is something noble about putting aside her own crap and diving headlong into this persona of "fineness."

As the week wears on, Max tapes up a picture of

Chancellor Merkel next to Cate to remind herself that great leaders put on brave faces for their populaces. How would a war work if platoon commanders started sobbing—and they must be totally tempted—the minute they heard gunfire? Be the change you want to see in the world—even if you're now questioning if that change is possible, you know, for everyone.

On Saturday afternoon, Max is trying to feel inspirational as she waits for Bridget in the understated armor of her Lululemon jacket, standing clear of the tourists sightseeing before the Halloween Parade. In contrast to their boisterous enthusiasm, Bridget is easy to spot. She walks over to Max in a gray sweater and leggings a half pace slower than the crowd.

"Hi," she says as if the syllable takes enormous effort.

"Okay, put some floppy ears on you, and you could go as Eeyore."

The corners of Bridget's mouth don't quite turn all the way up, but they look like they're considering it. "Taylor and I have gone trick-or-treating since we were kids. It was our holiday. Look, I'm showered. I'm dressed. I'm trying."

Max puts her arm around her. "I know. And today we're going to take that to the next level. Come on." Max steers her across Broadway through a gaggle of girls emerging from their dorm, their night of party-hopping starting early.

"Naked is not a costume," Bridget says, her hands whipping up.

"Right?" Max concurs.

"I mean, hello?" Bridget looks back over her shoulder at the fishnet-cloaked ass cheeks. "How is it appropriate to be outside dressed like you're headlining a strip club?"

Max laughs as she points to their destination a few doors down. "Right? Where's the creativity?" Bridget smiles back as Max holds the glass door to the industrial foyer. "Okay," Max announces, "here we are. Molinaro's Gym." Max presses for the elevator just as the stairwell slams open and a guy who looks like Taylor at twenty blows out, skateboard in hand. Bridget's face goes slack again.

"Bridget?" Max beckons her into the car.

"Yes?"

"Okay, let's take a little victory lap." Bridget looks questioningly at her as the door slides shut. "Tiny. The size of this elevator." Max extends her pointer fingers at shoulder-height. "Yay," she whispers before putting her hands on Bridget's shoulders. "That minute on the way in here when you were smiling about slutty Halloween costumes? That was your window of euphoria. It may not feel like much. But it's a start."

The elevator pings, and they get off onto the gym floor. A boxing ring sits in the middle, surrounded by sweaty guys sparring in head protectors. The man behind the counter nods to Max, and she leads Bridget straight into the women's locker room—a makeshift space behind a curtain the management had to add a few years ago when they discovered a clientele demanding an outlet for this new "girl power."

"Boxing?" Bridget asks skeptically while they take off their jackets. "Really? Taylor doesn't love me anymore, I projectile-snotted on him when he told me, but I'm going to hit a bag of sand, and that'll make it all better?"

Max pulls out a set of gloves and a roll of cloth. "Hold out your hands." Max carefully mummifies Bridget's knuckles and then slips on her gloves. "Pink—cute, right?"

"Ma-ax," Bridget says, her Eeyore intonations returning.

"Come on." She leads Bridget out to the large bag dangling from an exposed I beam in the ceiling. "Okay, stand with your feet apart, right one slightly in front, bend your knees a little. This is your power base—you've just lowered your center of gravity, making you harder to knock down. This is what the program is all about—making you harder to knock down."

"Next time," Bridget adds.

"Next time," Max concedes.

"There will never be a next time," Bridget wails.

"Bridget! No crying in boxing. Okay, face the bag, pull back with your right arm, and punch."

"Punch?" Bridget asks disbelievingly, her arms hanging limply at her sides.

"Punch!"

Bridget taps the bag.

"Bridget," Max asks patiently. "How you feelin'?"

"Like that elephant isn't just standing on my chest, it's taking a crap."

Yep, Max thinks, *that's about it.* "Okay, that's vivid. Now, who made you feel that way?"

The corners of Bridget's eyes wet. "I lost him. I'm alone and sad because I did something wrong—I don't know what—I've replayed it and replayed it."

"You're alone—and you're not alone by the way—you have friends—because Taylor blew it. Because he was selfish and self-centered and treated a couture girlfriend like she was an Old Navy tank top. You are special. One of a kind! And it's time to get angry. Punch, Bridget."

She pulls back and gives a little wallop. The bag doesn't move.

"Okay," Max says, "I was hoping not to have to do this." She reaches into her bag and pulls out the teddy bear Taylor won for Bridget at the San Gennaro festival.

"My zeppole bear!"

"What did he say when he handed this bear to you?" Max prompts, already knowing the answer from Shannon.

"He said he loved me."

"And?"

"Kenyon wasn't too far, and even when he went to college he'd come back to visit." Bridget spins to the bag and strikes with all of her might.

"Yes!" Max cheers her on as Bridget pummels the bag, her rage coming to the surface. She doesn't notice Max's own face go red as she thinks back to a similar whispered promise. . . .

"I missed you," Hugo had said into her bare neck beneath the covers of his bunk bed. "Thanksgiving sucked. Everybody saying the same stupid things to each other. You would've hated it."

"I'm sure," Max had responded, having no idea. Hers involved a six-hour delay for a three-hour flight to Tampa, a one-bedroom condo, her father's new girlfriend, who couldn't cook, but that was okay because, "That's not what Thanksgiving is really about." Uh, yeah, *it is.*

Three days of dying to get her dad alone—even just for a walk around the complex's pool. A walk that never came. And then an even longer delay on an even longer flight back.

"What are you doing for Christmas?" Hugo asked between kisses of her ear.

"New York," she said, hoping it sounded glamorous.

"Oh God, with all the tourists?"

"I guess so," she said nervously, not sure where she fell on the subject. Her mother had called to proudly share she had just moved into her boyfriend's town house in Brooklyn, but this would be Max's first visit to the city.

"You should see Haven," he pronounced with finality. "You'd get a kick out of it."

"Who?" Max felt forced to admit her ignorance, hoping it would come off as endearing.

"Our place on the Cape." Hugo readjusted their position so she lay beside him in his arms. "It's beautiful at Christmas. Caroling, midnight mass, followed by champagne. Some of the tradition can get a little tedious, but . . ."

"Mmm, that sounds . . . perfect," Max agreed as she wondered if he meant it. She *should* see it, like, she should learn a foreign language or she's invited?

"You'd love it."

She would, she was sure of that. She would love a lot

of things. "Mmm." Max repeated the noise in the hopes that it didn't sound like either accepting an unextended invitation or rejecting a real one.

He put his arms behind his head. "I get it. Christmas is family—ritual, routine, whatever. But maybe you can come for New Year's?"

"Yes," she said without hesitating, sitting up, her hands on his bare chest. "Yes!"

She didn't know then what she knows now, that less than a year later he would just be a stranger—

"He—" Thwack. "Said—" Oof. "We—" Thud. "Were—" Pow. "Soul mates."

Twenty minutes later Bridget is soaked in sweat—and grinning. "That was amazing," she says as Max holds out a water bottle. "I never got boxing. Now I *totally* get it. A charge goes up your whole arm. It's like hooking up."

"I've bought you a ten-class pass so you can come back whenever you need. Plus I got you a DVD to do at home. Even striking air can feel awesome when you put intention behind it." Max sees Bridget to the elevators and then hangs back with the pink gloves. She is feeling the urge to pummel the niggling uncertainty about her future, which Hugo is triggering. She strides back to the studio, where the bag still sways slightly from Bridget's fury.

Her phone pings with a text—from Ben, her new friend. "Party 2nite @ Soho House, 10 p.m. If I have 2 be there so do u." She smiles.

While she's wrapping her hands, her phone pings with three more successive messages: A client who's crashing after bingeing on her family's candy supply and can't stop crying. A client who's found herself outside her ex's house with a carton of eggs and just needs to throw them at his window *so badly*. And a client whose friend is about to become a client after her ex just uninvited her from his Halloween party on Facebook and then changed his status to "single."

A trainer offers to secure Max's gloves for her. "You wanna use the bag?" he asks.

She shakes her head—there's no time. She peels the strips back off and returns them to her tote for her next client, knowing she is needed elsewhere. "No. Thanks, though." Max hustles to the elevator. "I'll have to wait."

By the time Max is finally able to start getting ready, the sun has long set on Ex, Inc.'s first Halloween day and she is wondering if—just like therapists notoriously dread what Christmas does to their patients—in time, her work may kill her previous love of the holiday. Every year Halloween was always an awesome night out with her new friends—the event when Max made it into their group photos, the ones that would get framed or taped up onto bedroom walls. Now she needs a night out with an old one. Zach has been coolly businesslike with her in the last few weeks. They need to cut off from work and hang out. The destination will be the Meatpacking District. She's read about the private club Ben invited her to in *Us Weekly*, but never imagined she might go there. Apparently the manager has a kid in Ben's class. And it's just a few short blocks from NYU. The perfect opportunity, Max realized, to show that she can live her life in Hugo's vicinity and be full-out fine.

After Max sprays her last curl into place and zips up her costume, she reaches into her bustier to make sure her cleavage is at full effect. Then she carefully applies the finishing touches to her eye makeup, looking frequently to the tip sheet she taped to the mirror. In the reflection she catches the fifth step up on the staircase, the one with the loose board under which sits the shoe box. Inside which is a picture of her and Hugo team-dressed as Harry Potter and Voldemort. Which, in that blahtastic community, was a big statement. Even if it wasn't Kate Middleton and Prince William like she'd suggested. And then, her memory is overtaken. She recalls kissing Hugo with such fervor that his costume glasses broke—

She snaps the lid shut on her Cyber Gold eye-shadow compact with too much force. She shakes her head as if the memories could literally fly loose out of her ears and be swept up, with the fumbled false-lash attempts, into the trash.

Halloween night is disarmingly warm this year, making the streets extra clogged with revelers, and Max is relieved to finally be ushered into Soho House's lobby by the bouncer. Zach is Iron Man, his boyfriend, Tom, is Thor, Phoebe is Black Widow, and Josh is Captain America. Max, in protest that Marvel Comics are so pin-headedly dude-heavy, is Wonder Woman. Maybe she doesn't have her own movie *yet*, Max thinks, but she's a perennial classic. And she already owned the red boots.

Yes, okay, so *maybe* she accounted for "living her life in his vicinity" in her costume. But it's not like it's lingerie. It's not like her ass cheeks aren't covered. Like trying to look her most fabulous best means anything. Full-out fine doesn't mean frumpsville.

The super posse steps off the elevator on the sixth floor and almost trips over an honest-to-God full-sized gondola. Zach reads the welcome sign posted on the wall above the pumped-in fog. "The theme is a Venetian masked ball."

Max looks through the French doors into the party and sees that everyone is wearing a mask, making finding

Ben a challenge. Not to mention that if Hugo is here he could walk right up to her and she wouldn't even know it. She feels that roiling suck of anxiety wetting her crimson heels. But this is Halloween—there are no masks in college, she reminds herself, unless she takes some freaky theater class and the chances of Hugo taking some freaky theater class are—oh, what the hell does she know anymore, it's probably his new pastime. He's probably majoring in business, minoring in mime.

"SHAKE IT!" Zach exhorts her as he slips into the crowd in his skintight red jumpsuit, the porniest take on Iron Man imaginable. She quickly shoots Ben a text with her location. Katy Perry comes on, and Max gives Zach a thumbs-up, wedging onto the floor with Phoebe and Josh, throwing herself into the music, willing this to be a night to be framed.

But finally she can't take it anymore, the holding her spine a little too straight, the self-consciousness that her dancing has to be Beyoncé backup worthy, the constant effort of keeping her boobs safely confined in her eagle-embroidered bustier. She gestures to the neon sign for the restrooms and heads off.

She is just reapplying her lip gloss when Zach comes out of the stall behind her. "Um, hey, party crasher," Max says, pointing at him with the wand.

"Now, you don't mind little ol' me, do you, ladies?" Zach asks the primping crowd and they all smile, amused. He spins to Max, leaning a hip against the tiled sink counter. "Tom is breaking my heart."

"What?" Max asks, her hands flying to her own.

"No, no, not like that."

"Zach," she admonishes, "you cannot use that phrase casually with me. It's like telling a cop Tom is trying to kill you."

"But he is! He has been bumping and grinding with that Care Bear for an hour!"

"Five minutes—tops. But if it bothers you, Zach, tell him."

"I can't crowd him!"

"Don't make yourself miserable trying to be Perfect Boyfriend. If he's doing something that bums you out, give him the opportunity to change. Because if you don't—and then you dump him—"

"I'm no better than any of our clients' exes," Zach says, finishing her sentence.

"Yes."

Zach kisses her on the cheek with a loud smacking sound. "You're so right. You're always so right!"

Feeling good to be right, she slips her arm around his waist as they step back into the chaos—the mob of masked revelers—the acrobats dressed like

Harlequins—the strippers dressed like courtesans—
when out of the corner of her eye she sees a tall, blond
guy wearing a Donald Trump mask and instinctively
yanks Zach to a crouch behind a purple velvet sofa. They
both look in shock to where her nail has snagged his red
suit. Forcing herself, Max stands and cranes her head.
The blond walks past—not Hugo. Bad move. So very,
very bad. Zach climbs back up, and they look into each
other's eyes. "I need some air." She turns before he can
respond, pushing away to the far wall and then inch-
ing along until her hand feels a doorknob. It opens to a
stair landing, and she quickly descends a floor to a door
marked LIBRARY. *That sounds quiet,* she thinks.

It turns out to be a large, ironically book-free room,
crisscrossed with tufted leather couches and anchored by a
long zinc bar at its far end. The lights from the neighborhood pour in from the windows, and Max feels no need
to flick on the lamps as she drops onto a couch, letting
her shoulders slump, her décolletage sink, her skin dry.
She unzips her boots and lifts out her feet. She feels the
point of her crown digging into her forehead and flings
it off. Then she reaches under her perfect barrel curls to
where the layers of Elnett are making her itchy and gives
her scalp a good scratching, instantly feeling better.

From across the room Ben watches Max, wondering
if he should announce himself before she fully disrobes.

He's always wondered if any of those getups girls wear on Halloween are comfortable. He knows he's supposed to be blinded by the display of thigh and boob, but every Triple-X Bo Peep he passes he just thinks, *That looks like it's digging into you somewhere.*

"I was just checking my phone." He tugs at his bow tie as Max whips her head up. Ben sticks his hand out from the wingback chair and waves, suddenly happy that Taylor guilt-talked him into staying out.

"Oh my God, are you watching me scratch my head like a deranged chimpanzee?"

"Did you get my text—we ran late. Which kind of sucks because I have to be up and taking on my future at the ass crack of dawn." He crosses to her while she pulls out her phone.

"Oh, sorry, I didn't feel it vibrate. Probably because the whole floor upstairs is. That sucks about your seminar tomorrow. Can I recommend espresso? I think those energy drinks are gonna bore holes in you. And it's the hair spray—it makes me itchy."

"I've heard," he says as he sits next to her behind the oversized coffee table.

"Oh?"

"Friend's little sister, takes ballet, comes home, and scratches out her bun until she looks like Einstein."

Max smiles, finally feeling comfortable for the first time all night. "How's your Halloween going?"

Ben reaches into the pocket of his tuxedo jacket and pulls out a box of Dots, two Snickers, and a Reese's Peanut Butter Cup. "Best costume ever. I'm only wearing ones with pockets from now on."

"And who are you supposed to be?" she inquires as she rips the wrapper off one of the Snickers.

He slides a mimed pistol from the breast pocket of his tux and pivots. "Bond."

"Original."

"My friend's idea. He's wearing garbage. Together we're junk bonds."

She smiles. "You definitely got the better end of the costume."

"I borrowed it from my dad—there's still rice in the pocket from his wedding." He pulls out a couple of grains.

"To your mom?" she asks. "Do you mind if I . . . ?" She gestures to her side zipper.

"Be my guest. Yeah, they split last year."

"Ahhhh." Max inhales deeply as her ribs fluff and resume their rightful place. She holds the front of her corset up with her forearm. "At least yours were married. My parents were a grad-school fling."

"Wow."

"Yeah. They get along pretty well, considering they were practically strangers thrown into the joint project of raising a human."

"Where's your dad?" Ben asks, unwrapping the Reese's.

"Florida."

"And you get to visit him?"

Max nods.

"I'm jealous. Other than overnights for baseball, I've never gone anywhere."

"Where do you want to go?" She reaches to dislodge a wad of caramel from her molar.

"Everywhere."

"Me too. Eventually. But strictly places they write guidebooks about. No one has written *Fodor's Wichita* or *Let's Go Buffalo!*"

Ben laughs.

"Next year you'll be somewhere brand-new, right?" she asks.

"Yeah, I guess," he says, realizing, compared with how intriguing everything about hanging with Max feels, the comfort of Kenyon is feeling less appealing with every passing week. "So why're you disrobing in an empty room?" Ben changes the subject, again pushing the thought of his known future away.

"Well, I tried to disrobe upstairs—make some extra cash—but no one was having it."

"Fools," he says, allowing his eyes to drop for an instant to where the curve of her breast is visible in the gape at her side. Wondering if he was a moron not to ask her out on a date when they first met. Now they're falling into the friend box, and it would be weird. Mostly, as he watches her lick at a stray string of caramel, he just wants to kiss her. Wants to take her face in his hands and plant his mouth on hers, let her arms find the back of his neck, her top falling down—

"Ben?"

"What?"

"I asked why you were sitting in the dark."

He can't tell her the truth. "My friend kind of has social ADD right now. He, like, can't sit still. He thinks *Maxim*'s Hot One Hundred are going to be at the *next* high school house party. We've trucked through six places tonight—and all I have to show for it is candy. He wouldn't even let me slow down to take a leak. So when he wanted to leave here for some party uptown I was just like, dude, I've got an early morning." And, really, even though he should be heading home, he had to wait to see if Max texted back.

"Now you're stuck here with me." She twists her red lips in a smirk.

That does it. Not letting himself think himself out of it he leans forward—

"Max!" Zach bursts in, trailed by Tom, Phoebe, Josh, and every other Marvel character they found upstairs. "We're avenging the crowding and creating our own *private* party! Woo-hoo!" Ignoring her dishabille, Zach leaps up onto the coffee table. She smiles in gratitude as he makes an instant dance floor for her to enjoy herself unobserved. Knowing Hugo would never let himself be seen in a comic book costume—even if he might want to.

Phoebe goes over to a sound panel in the wall and somehow turns on the speakers, accessing the system upstairs. Pink asks everyone to raise their glass. "Would you?" Max asks in turn, pointing down. Ben zips her boots while she tugs up her top. She holds out her hand, forcing herself not to be the other take on her costume—not to *wonder*—even for a second—if Ben Cooper was about to kiss her.

She tugs him onto the coffee table, finally *really* giving over to the music, getting sweaty, mussing her hair, making pouty faces with Phoebe and Zach—the respite lasting exactly four songs. Word of the party-within-the-party spreads, and just as Max throws her hands up to Alejandro, the masked-many fill the room around them, crashing their sanctum. Max's looping mental track of *isthathim?isthathim?isthathim?* resumes, making it impossible for her to stay on the beat. Seemingly

oblivious, Ben smiles at her as he swings his blazer overhead, but all she can think is that, at NYU, no matter
what great friends she makes, what fabulous parties they
go to, what pouty faces they share—Hugo will always
maybe be there, making it impossible to even begin to
think about other very charming—and actually very
cute—boys who might want to kiss her.

CHAPTER 8

"A speed bump." Max assesses Bridget's crisis a few evenings later from Bridget's living room. "That's all this is." Having doffed her parka, Max slides her spine down the frame of the picture window that looks out on Bank Street, the cause of Bridget's 911 text.

"Speed bump?" Bridget snaps from where she hides behind a cabinet door in the open kitchen, all lights extinguished because of Taylor's decision to spend the day hanging around his front stoop with his buds. Any movement Bridget makes is visible through that picture window, which takes up almost the entire front wall of the Stetsons' ground floor.

"Okay, a road block," Max concedes in the dark, tapping her cell on her tucked knees, her brow furrowing as the skateboarding boy-shaped shadows zip back and forth across the room.

"I'm being *held hostage.*"

"How's your happy place?" Max asks, despite that there's no denying hers will now be known as: Place She Will Spend Four Years Covered in Flop Sweat and Hiding in a Crouch. "Om?"

"He's skating on it." But at least Taylor will graduate high school and leave. Hugo has barely unpacked.

"Okay. Taylor's been outside since when?"

"Noon. It's *nine.* Taylor's been racing around in front of my house on that crap skateboard for nine hours. They closed off the block for a street stoop sale. What's everyone selling? Don't know because *I've been in here*! For *nine hours*! Punished because my parents, who are happily enjoying the ballet, don't believe in drapes! Trapped in darkness since the sun went down! And with your stupid rules about running into him, I missed the street sale, my cousin's birthday, and now *Project Runway* night. Toss whatever transportation metaphors you want at it, just get—me—out—of this—house."

From the street, the whirring gathers in volume, erupting in a clatter and a round of, "Dudes!" from

Taylor's friends. Max watches Bridget hit her breaking point, her palms pushing into the sides of her head
like she's attempting a "My Name Is Pudgy" face. Max
doesn't bother assessing Taylor's friends in any detail. The
point is there's a potential audience. "Bridget . . ." Max
buys time. "I'm just highlighting the larger truth here, in
general you're moving in a forward direction. This may
feel like a setback—"

"This feels like torture."

"But so do the SATs! And they're moving you forward, out of high school. What we need to do . . ." Max
drops below the sight line of the window ledge, which sits
all of two feet from the floor, and crawls around the couch
to the kitchen island. She pictures herself doing the same
thing across the floor of the NYU student center.

"What we need to do?" Bridget prompts from where
she stands above.

"What we need to do is, um, not be . . ." Max reaches
a hand up, and Bridget pulls her to her feet. "Demoralized." The two stare across the dim living room, out to
where Taylor and his untiring crew are upgrading their
skate ramp with a second trash can.

"I'm demoralized."

"Bridget."

"I am. That un-helmeted redhead used to cry before
going to sleep because he loved me so much he couldn't

handle it. Now he doesn't care if I live or breathe, and I'm the one trapped in the dark. In the dark, Max!"

"You were going to a *Project Runway* night. At whose house?"

"Lindsay's. Now her and Shannon will just—"

"You're hosting." She puts her cell in Bridget's hands. "Call Shannon. It's good for him to get a hit of you just hanging out, and this is the perfect opportunity. Now, where's your TV?"

An hour later, Max puts the finishing touches on Bridget's Pure Color no-makeup makeup and turns her freshly applied healthy glow to the upstairs bathroom mirror.

"Wow, I look happy," Bridget murmurs.

"Now imagine what you'll look like smiling." Max twists the top back into the mascara.

"Me next!" Lindsay, who Bridget has sworn up and down can be trusted, jockeys for the toilet-lid-cum-spa-chair. "This is so cool! It's like we're Mr. and Mrs. Smith."

"We need to keep moving, Lindsay. Okay, guys—" Max turns to point the gold tube at the tiled wall as if it's a map of the country they're about to invade. "To review: Lights on! Down the stairs. Bridget to the phone, call the pizza place. Lindsay, you and Shannon chill on the stools at the island while she orders. Then Shannon pours drinks, Bridget grabs snacks. Lindsay, plates and napkins, and then everyone casually reconvenes in the basement rec room. Questions, comments, concerns?"

Bridget tugs at a lash as Lindsay suggests, "We could dance around the island lip-synching into a spatula?"

Max spins to Bridget. "That is not happening tonight. Oh God, or ever." Max shudders.

"Listen to Max like she's the Bible, Bridge," Shannon encourages as they follow Max down the hall. "If she says lip-synch, you ask what tune."

"Which I'm not saying," Max repeats for clarification as nerves are running high.

"How many more weeks until Bridget has her Moment?" Shannon presses her lips together to refresh her Electric Ginger gloss—the hue that Max had picked out for her when they did her Moment, two months ago, for Todd Clark.

Max considers how Bridget's prep has been going. "We haven't selected the activity yet, but, if we get nothing else out of tonight, I'm ready to start her on skateboard lessons tomorrow. She's getting close. She's moving *forward*. Because today is not a what, Bridget?"

"U-turn? Lane merge?" Bridget, approaching the top step, shakes her hands at the wrist and cracks her neck to loosen up as she does before each basketball game.

"A setback. Okay!" Max steps down a stair to take stock while the three line up. Looking them over, she does a quick fly-pulled-up, hair-smoothed-down check. "And . . . action."

Max flips the switch. The fixture over the stairs comes to life, illuminating the girls as they descend the worn runner a little too fast. "And kitchen light on—good, good." Following her mandate to remain invisible to clients' exes, Max inches down as she directs from the blind spot created by the vestibule. "You're grabbing the phone there on the counter, Bridget—don't freeze—turn to your friends. Friends, you're not standing, you're sitting on stools. Not like there's guns at your backs—casual—more casual—slouch. Slouch! Somebody say something, talk to Bridget." Max leans forward to see that the lights have drawn the attention of the guys, who glance over from where they're taking a break on Taylor's stoop. "Lindsay, Shannon, loosen her up. Say something, anything!!"

"Anything!" Shannon says shrilly.

"I forgot who I'm calling." Bridget turns the color of the tomato dish towel hanging on the oven. "Who am I calling?!"

"Pizza," Lindsay says through clenched teeth.

"Bridget." Max aims for calm. "This isn't the opening scene of a *Scream* movie, just dial the pizza place."

Bridget's knuckles whiten around the phone. "Forgot the number. Can't think of the number. Oh my God, I can't do this. Is he watching? Just tell me. *Is he?!*"

"Call 411," Max urges. "*Talk to each other.* Recite a poem, anything—they can't read your lips."

"I'm gonna pee," Lindsay warns.

And because she looks like she very well might, Max drops to her stomach and snakes the floor to arrive beneath their stools. Six saucer-sized eyes stare down at her. "Don't!" Their faces shoot to the ceiling. "Not up! At each other! Look at each other, interact! Oh my God, Bridget *TALK*!"

"Hil'dliketoplaceanorderfordelivery?"

When finally in the sanctity of the basement's windowless rec room, all three girls face-plant on the tan sectional, utterly drained. "How'd that go?" Bridget asks into the cushion.

"Great, really great." Max flops back on the couch.

"Don't even want pizza now," Shannon moans.

"Shut up, when do you not want pizza?" Bridget pushes herself to sitting.

"True." Shannon tugs the box down the coffee table and opens the lid.

"That was so intense." Lindsay queues up the DVR.

"I think I aged, like, ten years waiting for that frickin' delivery guy to show."

"But, wow, do you guys really know your alphabet," Max marvels.

"Lip-synching would have been easier." Bridget twists her hair over her shoulder before handing a slice to Max. "Here's the game—every time Tim Gunn says, 'Make it work' everyone screams, and when Heidi says, 'You're either in or you're out' we have to switch seats before the whole phrase is out of her mouth."

"It's a little middle school, but it passes the time," Shannon adds, dabbing a napkin at the grease dripping down her chin.

"Thanks, but I should let you guys—"

"Because in fashion, you're either—"

"Move it!" Shannon calls over Heidi, inciting a scramble to reseat.

"You're a natural, Max." Bridget reaches to retrieve her plate of pizza from the other side of the table.

When Max says good-bye on Bridget's doorstep at the episode's end, the street is clear of any evidence of Taylor's impromptu skate-a-thon. While Shannon and Lindsay pile three bowls with ice cream in the kitchen, Bridget pulls Max into a quick hug. "You saved me—again,"

Bridget exclaims as she braces the door open.

"It's what I do." Max smiles, pulling Peter's parka back on.

"Yeah, what else do you do?" Bridget leans against the door frame. "I mean, when not being Wonder Woman." She points at the wallpaper she noticed on Max's phone, which displays a shot of her crew before they hit Soho House.

"Oh, you know, I have my research—"

"But do you go out?" Bridget asks in a way that lets Max know she's really been mulling it over. "I meant *out* out. Like, with guys. Like hooking up."

"Oh! I mean, it's challenging with my work schedule. Sure, yes. Totally. I totally go out with guys. All the time."

Bridget glances over her shoulder at her chatting friends and steps closer to Max, dropping her voice. "I figured if *you* were going out, then there's hope for me. Obviously you lived through someone like Taylor at some point and obviously you're more than fine; you're, like, perfect. But I couldn't tell if you'd, you know, if you'd been in love again."

Max feels a sickening twist beneath her ribs. "Of course! Yeah, a ton of times," Max says too quickly. She's seventeen; "a ton" sounds ridiculous.

"Good!" Bridget hugs her sweater to her chest, her

face breaking open in relief. "That's so good to hear. I just really need to know that when I'm done with your program, I'll stop feeling so I-see-your-face-in-my-dreams about Taylor. Stop being attracted to him." Bridget's eyes dart up to Max's, having arrived at the truth of her concern. "I will stop, won't I?"

"Absolutely! Ex, Inc. has a one hundred percent success rate. Every single girl who has completed the program through her Moment honestly couldn't care less about her ex."

"Including you?"

Up until she saw Hugo again Max would've jumped to reassure Bridget. She would have said, *Oh my God, girl, he could plant one on me and I'd rather be watching Gaga on YouTube.* But now it's impossible to gloss over Max's own recovery, or lack thereof, so breezily. "Look, just because you're still attracted to Taylor doesn't mean the program isn't working—or you're not healing."

"It doesn't?" Bridget sounds understandably underwhelmed.

"No . . . no. That attraction . . . that's just chemical. Hormonal jet lag. It doesn't necessarily mean he's your soul mate—" Blessedly, Max's phone starts to ring.

"Next call?" Bridget asks.

"Yes." Max lays her palm on Bridget's crossed arm. "Focus on tonight's success, not the post-hookup cling of that sweaty ass ball across the street. Ten hours of rolling back and forth twenty feet on a board, culminating in hurling himself over a recycling bin? Really, Bridget, this is the love of your life? Father of your kids? Man to grow old with?"

Bridget doesn't answer.

"Gotta run. Hey, you're either in or you're—"

"Out!" Bridget flicks a finger in the air as Max finally answers her phone.

A few blocks later, Max has instructed Phoebe to freeze a client's car keys in water rather than risk her using her learner's permit after dark for another "casual drive-by." She slows beneath the light of a newsstand to slide her phone into her purse, her eye caught by the banner on the Page Six supplement of the *New York Post*. REAL ESTATE ROYALTY SHOPPING BIG APPLE FOR HIS PRINCESS! And there's Hugo with some blond nestled against him as they dodge past velvet ropes. Max lunges for the paper, but it's impossible to see the girl's face. She scans the paragraph, but there's no name. Shopping for his princess?! A girlfriend? Now Max has to be in class with Hugo and a girlfriend?! Okay, that's just too much. She needs to talk about this roadblock, speed bump, setback, whatever. *What* is she going to do? She returns the paper and calls Zach.

"Max?" he yells over very loud music.

"Zach? Can you talk?"

"Max?"

"Yes, can you talk?"

"Can't hear you! I'm at a concert with Tommy. Will you be up in two hours? Don't answer. Can't hear. I'll call in two!"

The line goes dead. Max wishes she could just get on Facebook and connect with old friends—but she doesn't begin to know how to catch anyone up to the point where she can ask advice. She was never great with keeping in touch with everyone. On to the next school, the next ecosystem she had to harness all her resources for fitting into.

She sees the subway entrance looming at the block's end, its green light hovering above two women standing close together. One can barely get through her story they are laughing so hard, holding on to each other. Max pulls out her phone and finds herself texting the one person she suddenly really wants to talk to. "Cooper baby, any chance ur out? Don't feel like going home yet. M."

When Max hits SEND, Ben is stuck at his grandfather's retirement home in Bay Ridge trying desperately to uncover a dark family secret. Any dark family secret. A bit of disturbing Cooper lore that Ben could have learned "in his youth" that "facing" made him become a "better, more interesting person." A person somehow differentiated from everyone else filling out the common app.

"Bro, you called me." Taylor's voice pulls Ben back from rereading Max's text.

"Sorry, that girl, Max, just texted. She wants to hang out."

"Yeah?"

"I'm not exactly next door, though." Ben looks around the small suite set up to feel as much as a home as humanly possible—and failing. "What are you up to?" he asks.

"Just, uh, watching Bridge. She was hanging out with some friends. She's gone now. Or upstairs. The house is dark again. Sorry, you were saying?" Taylor asks, and Ben hears the clank of Taylor's bedroom blinds hitting the sill.

"Bridget? Why are you watching her? You two hanging out again?" Ben asks, surprised as he hops up to sit on the two feet of counter.

"No. Just, I don't know, usually when it's over with girls there's more of a mess and she's been—not one. I haven't seen her at all, and then tonight I saw her hanging. I mean, I've kinda been thinking about how she always used to do this cute thing where she'd bite the tip of her tongue when she was concentrating. Whatever. It's just I'd heard she was chill, and she looked . . . chill."

"So you're watching her?" Ben waves a hand in the air, trying to get Taylor to the point.

"What's fun in Denture Land?" Taylor asks, and Ben realizes he's changing the subject. "Find your inspiration?"

"Nah, it's all like I've always heard. His dad came from the Old Country. They changed his name from Capernico at Ellis Island. He worked his ass off, married my great-grandma, started the store—"

"Didn't secretly go back and fight for Mussolini?"

"Dare to dream."

"Store basement wasn't a stop on the underground railroad?"

"I wish."

"Bummer. Look, I think you're sweatin' this way too much. I mean, the application isn't even due for another month and a half."

"Right," Ben says, unable to stifle his annoyance at Taylor's overconfidence.

"You want to swing by?" Taylor asks, and Ben hears the thud of the little basketball hitting Taylor's floor.

"I just said Max wants to meet up."

"Yeah."

"So if I can get back in time I'm going to meet up with her." Ben goes ahead and lays it out.

"I thought you and this chick are just friends."

"Dude, we are just friends." Ben feels himself get defensive.

"But you'd rather hang out with her?"

"What's your deal? You and I've been going out every night!"

"I'm just—I need you to be a friend right now."

"When am I not?" Ben asks as he overhears his exasperated grandfather saying his dad's name like he's still a kid. "I should go. My dad's trying to do some tax thing with him, and it's taking forever. Could you hook me up and call your dad's car service to come get me? It's my only chance of making it there."

"Dude, I don't know. I'm supposed to only use it for emergencies."

"You got them to take you ten blocks to the movies." Ben rests his hand on the refrigerator handle, the cold metal reminding him of the feel of Max's zipper as he slid it up her calf. "Come on, dude."

"You like her," Taylor says accusingly.

"No," Ben says, not ready to answer the question that will just lead to more questions. And humiliating answers. No, they haven't hooked up. No, he hasn't tried. No, he hasn't even asked her out.

"Admit you like her," Taylor challenges, "and I'll call them."

It's probably just as well that Ben couldn't hang out, Max thinks the next morning, or she would have slept late and missed this. She is nervous to be unexpectedly sitting across from her dad while he gets the check for the brunch they've shared at the glamorous Newark Airport Chili's before he goes through security. Her father had called when his flight from Chicago was rerouted to see if she wanted to meet during his delay.

Two subways, a train, and a tram later, she found him at Terminal B in his rumpled suit, waiting with the paper folded to the business section to give her one of his reassuring hugs.

They haven't been together since her ill-fated spring stay when she was still pulling herself up from her St. Something's tailspin. "Good to see you with an appetite." Her dad nods as she folds the last fry into her mouth. "You look great, Maxine. New York is really working for you."

"And I for it." She squeezes her knees under the table.

"So." He lowers his glasses to sign the bill. "How's

the school search going?" he asks. "Thought any more about the UCs? Your mom and I loved Berkeley. Think of all the sunshine. You could go to class and the beach on the same day."

"What would that outfit look like?"

"We've covered this." His face sets in seriousness. "You can't just apply to one school, Max. Not as a dropout. It's just not prudent. So there's NYU, but where else do you want to go?"

"How about nowhere?" There. She said it. It was one thing to be faced with Hugo. It's something else entirely to be faced, day in and day out, year in and year out, with Hugo in love with someone else. No matter how she's looked at it, she just can't figure out a way around this new reality. And she can't abandon her clients. So she'll just get an apartment and build her business the old-fashioned way. "I mean, the pioneers didn't have PhDs."

Her dad smiles like she's made a joke as he puts his card back into the worn slot in his wallet.

"I kind of mean it, Dad." She picks at the cocktail napkin under her sweating glass of orange juice, her mouth drying as she finally says it out loud. "I'm thinking about not going to school, like, at all."

"What?"

"Or at least taking a year off." And then another and another and another.

"Except you're having your year off. Isn't that what
we agreed? A year off and then college?" They stand
and he pulls on his blazer before putting his arm around
her shoulder and leaning into her ear. "You don't want
to be working here for the rest of your life, do you?"
They both watch a girl clear off the cheese-and-ketchup-
strewn plates into a gray bin with something miles below
enthusiasm. He turns his wheelie around to trail them
into the traffic heading to security.

"I could get an apartment of my own. We know Mom's
going to move on to another job any minute now. I just
can't imagine packing up again, Dad," she says, telling
him the least of what she can't imagine.

"That's because you have the wardrobe of a mid-
sized traveling circus. You sent me the financial planning
forms?" he asks. "Don't hit me with it all at once at the
zero hour."

"I did." She didn't. "Last week. Didn't you get them?"

"I'll ask Debbie. Maybe she saw them."

"Yes, ask Debbie. Maybe she used them to line her
bird's cage."

"It's a canary, Max. Come on, it's sweet."

"Except it's not," she says gently.

"I know," he concedes with a sigh. "But she is."

"Okay," Max says noncommittally.

They arrive at the long line of shuffling travelers

preparing to remove their belts and shoes. He pulls her into a hug, and she rests her head on his chest. "You're going to find a school you totally love, I know it. Boarding school is not college, Max. High school is not college. Nothing is." He hugs her. "I'll call you this week. Thanks for meeting your old man."

"Love you," she says as she backs up and turns to leave.

"Max!" he calls after her, and she spins around. "You're going to college."

Everyone in line is looking at her, and she sheepishly gives him a thumbs-up, having no freaking clue what she's going to do.

CHAPTER 9

Max feels like her brain is going to break open. Option A seems to be to go to NYU and forgo her fashions for a burka. Unappealing. Option B, go somewhere else and lose the opportunity to be mentored by Dr. Schmidt, the one woman who might see past her age and take Max's research seriously. Option C, forgo college altogether, build her business with grit and fortitude, and change the world with just a GED. Paternally vetoed. Which leaves Option D. As in doughnuts. Having motored through the gifts from her clients, Max has started making and frosting her own. At three a.m.

Understandably, given her lack of sleep, the week that ensues is an unmitigated mess. Sara's piñata came back as Minnie Mouse instead of a rat, and no matter how wounded a heart may be, no one can take a bat to Minnie. Max accidentally sent Phoebe to case a day care, whose name was one letter off from an ex's school. And the frozen car keys got served at the parents' cocktail party. And now it's Saturday, when, with no school to stifle the schedule, Ex, Inc. lines up doubleheaders.

Given how distracted Max's been, she's fully embracing the packed day because it allows no space for thinking about college or Hugo or his girlfriend or that the three subjects are now fused at the hip. Tanned, triangular muscles that narrowed into the band of his boxer shorts—would be an example of what she does not have the space to think about!

She's too busy wrangling a trio of Maltese in the late afternoon sun of Prospect Park. "How we doing, Zach?"

Zach shoots her a weary look from yards away, telegraphing how ballsy it is of her to inquire. He continues pep-talking Jess, whose Moment will showcase her newfound love of furry, four-legged creatures. Because her ex has three bullmastiffs, which, on the night he brought her home to meet his parents, bounded up, front paws on her shoulders, jowls splattering slobber, and humped her senseless. Jess informed Max that he never saw her the same after she screamed and slammed into their front door like a fly on a windshield. He dumped her within the week.

Unfortunately, Jessica's desensitization class, based on the principles of behavioral psychology, is taking twice as long as Max had anticipated, a miscalculation not lost on her annoyed staff. "Great! Let's go again."

Jess grips Zach's arm, which is already showing the flushing precursor to a bruise, as he walks her toward Max's neighbor's—Mrs. Denunzio—fluffy white dogs. All three strain to lick at Jess's approaching ankles. At the last second, Jess darts to the other side of the path, her arms overhead as if the puppies were bombarding her with mortar. "I can't! I can't!"

"Max." Phoebe drops her head back. "Isn't there something else she could do, something more achievable? Jump out of a burning building? Any chance her ex is also a pyro?"

"She's going to get this, Phoebe," Max reminds her through clenched teeth before turning to Jess with a calm smile. "You're going to get this. Look how much progress you made today!"

"Yes, I do recall." Zach's voice teeters on the edge of sarcasm. "When we got here you couldn't even come out from behind the tree." Jess nods from a safe distance.

Max takes a look at her watch. Michael Kors. Gold,

with a grounding masculine heft. It will *kill* her to give it back next week. "Yes. That's good for today. But awesome work, really awesome!" Max announces, hopefully covering her own disappointment. "Go home and watch *The Shaggy Dog*—with the sound *on* this time—and try to touch the screen at least once."

Jessica nods, takes a Fig Newton that Phoebe offers, and slumps off.

Zach and Phoebe drop on a bench, and Max has to dig deep not to join. "Okay!" Max punches the air as she invokes a rallying tone. Zach and Phoebe exchange looks. "Come on! Today's setback will only make Jessica's Moment feel all the more awesome when it does go perfectly—*as it will*. And Bridget will be here in five minutes so let's get moving. Break."

Zach and Phoebe push to their feet and move into setting up the next training. Within minutes the team has traded leashes for Airwalks as they suit Bridget up for her first skateboard lesson. Bridget seems blessedly unaware of the tension among those padding her. "There is no way I am going to—what did you call it?"

"Make him regret his entire existence," Max says as she adjusts Bridget's helmet.

"Yeah, that—in this getup. He can't even see me." She looks down at the plaid jacket and baggy cargo pants.

"But he'll see your moves." Max mollifies her. "You'll be like Hannah Teter. You'll rock his world. It'll be h-h-h-hot."

"I'm going to look like a dork. I'm going to eat it. It'll be l-l-l-lame."

"All right," Zach says, hopping on his board and making a slow run down the concrete path between the rows of splintering green benches. "Put your left foot on the board, transfer your weight to the left, and push, push, push off with your right, then bring your right leg in and gliiiiiiiide."

Bridget looks at him like he just gave her five easy steps to build a rocket and shakes her head.

"Bridget," Phoebe says firmly, "can we agree that the boys who devote their lives to this sport aren't exactly Nobel laureates? And if some tool whose idea of fun is misspelling 'cool' in spray paint can do this, you can, too."

"Okay, okay." Bridget takes a deep breath, sets her jaw, hops her left foot up—and the board goes out from under her.

"Or not," Phoebe mutters.

An hour later finds an officially alarmed Max inserting two chilled cans of soda down Bridget's pants to slow the swelling. "Do you think this is why they wear their jeans so baggy?" Bridget asks, wincing.

"So they can ice their asses with Mountain Dew? Maybe. Is that the spot?"

"Yes. Oh my God, I'm going to have to borrow my grandfather's hemorrhoid cushion. I'm not going to be able to sit down tomorrow."

"Start a rumor you're into spanking," Zach suggests as he peels a Mini Babybel, shot from hauling Bridget to her feet so many times.

Max widens her eyes at him to check his tone. "Zach, can you help Phoebe dismantle the ramp? I maybe set the bar a little high today." Zach gives her a "ya think" eyebrow raise as he heads down the path to Phoebe. "You okay?" Max asks. Bridget gestures to her rear with a look of disbelief. "I mean emotionally. You *can't* read anything into this. You're doing amazing on the program."

"Are you sure this skateboarding Moment thing is going to work?" Bridget pushes her waistband down a bit, and Max cringingly looks at where the skin is turning yellow. Why didn't she call her off twenty attempts ago?!

"Yes," Max promises.

"Because I *can't* keep feeling like this every day—right now I'd give anything to have early-onset dementia. This Moment has to work," Bridget says. "It *has* to. I'll do whatever it takes. I just can't spend the rest of my life seeing that expression on his face as I snotted." Max sees a virtually identical expression on Hugo's face and thinks a virtually identical thought about herself. "So be honest, Max, how did I look out there?"

"You looked like a dork," Max admits as much to Bridget as to her memory. "You ate it. It was l-l-l-lame."

Bridget laughs while Max forces herself to focus her remaining brain cells. Bridget. Bridget and Taylor. Baylor. "Okay. This hasn't been done before."

"What hasn't?"

"Switching Moments this close to deadline. But we need a Plan B." She waves Zach and Phoebe over. "You're not going to make anyone regret anything with your ass in a cast."

That night Zach drags his heels as he slowly packs up his Filson satchel with the day's files. Max chews at the inside of her cheek to keep from tugging off her clothes and hiding in the bathtub. She just needs this day—week—to be done. "You and Tom have fun tonight," Max says as she stands by her door, not so subtly tapping her foot.

"What? Oh. Well, he just admitted he doesn't like Ryan Gosling—we're working through it."

"There's always counseling," Max quips. "So, okay then, have a great night!"

He pauses reshuffling the already reshuffled papers and looks straight into Max's eyes. "We've *never* had to switch tracks on a Moment—"

"Zach, I've been juggling an unprecedented amount of cases. It'll be fine."

"And you still have perspective on what that is."

"Yes," she says faintly.

"And you'll solve Bridget's Moment in the next twelve hours."

"Of *course*." God willing. "Always have—always will."

He heaves the satchel over his shoulder. "Don't heart the idea of my Max losing her edge."

"Still edgy," she reassures him as he finally walks to the door. "See you tomorrow. Text me with any ideas."

He stops. "You know how I've been compiling the data on all our cases for your presentation to Professor Schmidt?"

"Yes?"

"I can't find Angie Riverdale's file." Zach reaches for his phone in his pocket. "And since she predates my employment, I wasn't sure if there's somewhere else I should be looking."

"Oh, right, I, um, took it out. The, uh, file," Max says with forced casualness of her only failure, the one client who sunk to depths even Ex, Inc. couldn't pull her from.

"You did?" He checks for texts and returns it to his bag.

"Oh my God, it was such a disaster. She, Angie, was a total aberration. Doesn't count. Don't give it—her—another thought."

"She shouldn't be included in the presentation?" He rests his hip against the wood.

"Nope." Max reaches around him for the knob. "Have a great night." She spins him onto the slate. "Call me about Bridget. Bye." She locks up and drops her forehead to the door, trying to steady her breath.

Her phone vibrates with the perfect distraction, a text from Ben. "SOS."

Ten minutes later, having tossed her hair into a ponytail and pulled on her Converse, Max is armed only with a tin of cookies from Trish Silverberg. She reads Ben's last text, checking his home address again as she walks the commercial stretch of Court Street. She's confused for a minute before she realizes where she must be headed. Just then the overhead lights at the back of Cooper Baby come on.

Ben unlocks the door and the bells jingle.

"Not what I pictured when you said you were home," she says, stepping inside, noticing he looks like he's been up for days.

Ben locks the door as Max takes off her coat. One track of her brain still poring over every word Bridget has uttered, the other circling around Zach's question like it's a maypole. "Dad lives upstairs. Mom kept the house over on Henry. Half the week I sleep here."

"Here?" Max asks, picking up a nursing bra from one of the overcrowded shelves.

Ben shakes his head, pushing his hands into the pockets of his sweats. "I have my own room, but it's hard to concentrate. This way."

Max follows him past the aisle of sippy cups and pacifiers to the back of the store, an open, carpeted space ringed with display strollers and high chairs. The floor is strewn with textbooks, soda cans, a laptop, all centered around a life-sized stuffed brown bear that has clearly been serving as a recliner.

"Shut. Up," Max says.

"It's for the toddlers," Ben explains, dropping onto the blue carpet and leaning against its massive trunk. "Surefire way to keep them occupied while their moms shop for number two or three."

"And it's just generally awesome," Max says, falling to her knees to stroke its soft arm.

"And it's just generally awesome," Ben agrees.

"You were reading by this?" Max asks, picking up

the glowing goose night-light. "No wonder you need a break."

He lifts his knees, resting his forearms atop them. "Didn't want to give the neighborhood the wrong impression—we'll have crazed moms with busted Sleep Sheep knocking on the glass in a minute."

"What's a Sleep Sheep?"

Ben hops up, goes to a shelf, pulls down a lamb in an open box, and presses its tummy. The sound of crickets fills the room.

"That is mad soothing," she acknowledges, cuddling the bear, an excellent stand-in for the bath she was planning on diving into. As her eyes drift closed, she thinks she should buy one of these for the baby, maybe just bring it downstairs for a couple of weeks first. "How do you get any work done?"

"Okay, where you see soft, furry awesomeness I just see a flashing neon sign that says 'Don't get stuck here, asshole.'"

"Right. Sorry." Max straightens up, deeply inhaling through her nose to revive herself. "What's the SOS?"

Ben looks down at Max, wondering why he didn't just let her fall asleep so he could watch her. Not creepily. That even sounded creepy in his own head. Not like that. Just . . . get to stare at *her* face without having to keep making sure *his* face doesn't look like it likes her. Does she know he almost kissed her at Halloween? Did she notice? Did she want him to?

"My brain is fuzzy. I just needed to talk to someone for five minutes, and everyone else is busy cramming for midterms and writing applications. My college essay sucks. I used all the pointers I got at that stupid seminar. But it still just . . . sucks."

"Hit me." Max opens the tin.

"You don't want to hear this crap."

"I do! It helps to read things out loud. I do it all the time. I'll think I have something all figured out, then read it aloud and hear the holes."

"Okay." Ben sits and scrolls to the top of the essay. "Just don't think I'm a moron. This is just a first draft."

"Peanut butter?" She passes him a cookie. "Has enzymes that build neurotransmitters—helps you think. And the sugar will keep you awake."

"Thanks." He smiles. "Okay, here goes." He clears his throat. "This is really embarrassing."

"Okay." Max considers what she's heard. "It's a frank opener."

"No—reading to you. Embarrassing that you're help-ing me with this." He gestures to the screen.

"Nah, please—it's what I do."

"Huh?" he asks.

"Be helpful." *At least I used to,* she thinks. "As a hobby," she covers. "Go ahead." She scrolls her hand at the wrist for him to continue.

"Okay." He looks down. More throat clearing. His face springs back up. "I don't even know where you go to school."

"I don't."

"You *don't*?" His eyes bug as he takes her in, suddenly making so much sense—and none at all. "Do you have, like, one of those hormone problems, like where you're really forty?"

"God, if only." She rolls her eyes. "No, I'm really only seventeen. Legal to drive—and not much else." She carefully brushes the crumbs back into the tin.

"Yeah," Ben says, commiserating. "So, why aren't you in school?"

"I finished early," she says simply.

"Shut up. You can do that?" He leans up to kneeling. "Are you, like, a genius? Did you graduate at ten? Are you already a doctor?"

She seems surprised to find herself laughing. "No, I am not middle-aged, nor am I a licensed professional. I just—needed to be done with high school." She shrugs, her face clouding. She picks a loose strand in the carpet.

"Wow. So what are you doing now? Are you gonna go to college?" Ben puts down his computer, his essay upstaged by this visitor from another planet.

"That would be the question." Max finds herself laughing again, this time more darkly.

"Don't you want to?"

"Yes. But only one school."

"Everyone has a first choice." Ben takes a cookie.

"No, an *only* choice. The Gallatin School at NYU. This professor I need to work with is there. It's the only place I'm applying."

"Your parents let you *do* that?" Ben asks, crumbs sprinkling the front of his sweatshirt.

"They don't know. They kind of have their hands full right now—what with the baby," she says, unable to keep the ouch from her voice.

"Yeah," Ben says, thinking back to last year, the basketball championship his dad spaced on, the teacher's conference his mom forgot. He gets it.

Max collapses fully on the bear to stare at the ceiling, letting her back arch, unaware her striped T-shirt is riding up to reveal her midriff, giving Ben that ache again.

"Okay, take it away," she says. In the glow of this little lamp, with this giant teddy bear and this nice guy at her feet, Max can feel herself getting dangerously close to asking his advice, which is idiotic because she hardly knows him. Maybe it's the hour or being in a baby store in the near dark, but it feels like she walked off the street and out of real life. Max starts mentally back at square one with Bridget to see where that gets her— Taylor likes Pop-Tarts . . . "Wow me. No pressure."

Ben pulls the MacBook back into his lap. "'I know what it is to be needed.'"

"Who said anything about needed?" Max replies.

"That's my topic sentence."

"Oh. Sorry. I love it."

"'I know what it is to be needed. My family has owned and operated a store in the same location since 1932. Originally my grandfather and great-grandfather hand made cribs and rocking horses. Now we sell everything a small citizen could need. Which means, in our insular neighborhood, we are there when people feel the most panicked and vulnerable. When they need their child's first thermometer or a pillow to help with colic.'" He looks up. "My guidance counselor told me to put in real examples. Lame?"

"No. Not at all—where's it going?"

Ben considers for a second, trying to put the idea that's been swirling around his mind into words. "It's about how I'm needed here—by the community, by my dad.

But I want college to show me the other ways I could serve, maybe ways I haven't thought of, ways that might make me—not my parents or my friends—happy." He stumbles on the last word.

She sees in his face for a split second such a genuine sadness it takes her breath away. She looks at Ben, really noticing him for the first time. *Was* he about to kiss her the other night? Did she want him to?

"Benjamin!" his father calls—Max can't figure out from where, his voice just sounds unsettlingly omnipresent. "Did you pick up my good suit from the cleaners?"

"Dad, Thanksgiving isn't for another two weeks! I'll get it!" Ben shouts at the fireproof tiles.

"I can't find it!"

"That's because it isn't here!" Ben shakes his head.

"Do you need to go upstairs?" Max asks.

"Nah. I used to think I had to be there all the time. He ate spaghetti every night."

"My dad still lives on omelets. He finally got a girl-friend—Debbie—but they do take-out. Your essay is going to be really good."

"Thanks."

"I totally get that. Wanting to serve. I found a way that makes me happy with my work. It's . . . this thing . . . that I can't really talk about." Max realizes this is the first time Ex, Inc. has come up when talking to a guy and that she has no idea how to even begin to explain it. "It's just making the college thing really stressful."

"It's intense," Ben says quietly.

She tilts her face inquiringly.

"This feeling that everything I do right now—every test I take, every paper I hand in, this essay . . . every choice I make between now and Christmas—will decide my life. Will determine if I get stuck like him or not," he blurts what he has tried pointlessly to put into words with Taylor.

Max nods as she looks at his face—she can see the band of tension above his eyes. "I didn't believe life worked like that, that it could all boil down to one thing. One choice."

"Didn't believe, as in past tense?" he asks. "What about now?"

She doesn't know.

He fidgets with his laptop, realizing how stupid this was inviting her over tonight—she's such a cool girl, she must see right through him.

"Sorry I wasn't much help," she says.

"No, no, I'm sorry I dragged you over here." He shuts his laptop. "Do you need me to walk you home?"

She reluctantly stands, hoping she hasn't said something

wrong. "I'm more likely to be mauled by that bear than hurt on the way to Clinton Street, but thank you."

"I just wouldn't want your boyfriend to come beat me up for letting you go unescorted." He wanted that to sound casual. It didn't.

"Boyfriend?" She shrugs on her puffer.

"I just, um, assumed you were, like, dating a DJ or something." Ben blushes.

"A DJ?" She laughs. "God, I don't know if I'm supposed to be flattered or insulted."

"My best friend thinks that is the only job worth having. He's talking about taking, like, classes on the weekend, I shit you not." He tries to shift them on to something, anything else.

They face each other by the plate-glass window, the light from the market across the street filtering through the mobiles as he realizes she hasn't answered his question.

Max's skin is prickling with excitement as Ben's comment makes her suddenly think of Taylor's skateboard. She's seeing it as if it were right under her nose, every sticker a band name. Of course, guys worship that scene! She wants to call Zach right now. She smiles as Ben opens the door, and before she realizes what she's doing she steps in to give him a hug. He holds her there, pulling her in tighter, and she lets her head rest—really rest—against the surprisingly solid warmth of his chest.

"You can do it," he murmurs into her hair.

"You too," Max says softly as she makes herself pull back, feeling suddenly shy. "'Night. Don't keep the bear up too late. He's probably a total asshole on no sleep."

He laughs, and she walks out onto Court Street.

CHAPTER 10

At 10:22 p.m. eastern standard time, Bridget's Moment is but a few away. Max is pumped like an athlete before an Olympic run. Because what is riding on tonight *feels* Olympian—regaining the confidence of her staff, pulling the recent string of client miscalculations from a nosedive, extinguishing plaguing doubt she can perform in New Hugo City (plus princess) and therefore go to New Hugo University (plus princess). No biggie.

Despite an impressive rally after the skateboarding debacle, the Ex, Inc. team is down to the wire. Max has claimed the supply closet of the Cabin, the hottest of hot clubs, as base camp for the night's operations. A former client's mom was the decorator, granting Max VIP access. Ex, Inc. then sent Taylor an official-looking invite and finagled him on the guest list.

The team arrived before opening to set up in the closet. After last August, when a client was shat on by a pigeon minutes before her Moment, forcing a full abort-mission, they now leave nothing to chance and always prep on site. Max is in cramped quarters, surrounded by cases of liquor and cocktail napkins, and is betting everything on an idea she actually got from Ben.

Her expression pensive, Phoebe withdraws her root beer lollipop from her mouth. "Her hair needs a few strategic waves," she says to Max as she finishes smoking Bridget's eyelids with Estée Lauder's Kajal Eye Crayon in teal. "It's sexy, but I'm filing a request for 'more.'" One would never guess from Phoebe's usually naked face, but she is a makeup wunderkind, just one of her many hidden and freakishly developed skills. Growing up, her bossy sisters usually commandeered the Barbies, leaving her to make the best of a dress-up box and Cray-Pas. Soon she could re-create anything she saw on TV.

"Denied," Max declares as she paces around them in the tiny space, mentally running through the plan like a figure skater prepping for the ice.

"But is it fabulous enough?" Zach asks doubtfully, sitting forward to get a closer look on the stool he's made from two crates of toilet paper.

"We're not going for fabulous," Max reminds them, her hands resting on the belt of her dress. "The fabulous is built in. We want Sam Ronson meets Charlotte Ronson. Casual, cool—and pretty. Bridget just stepped in off the street on any old random Thursday night, got asked to spin some tunes. She shrugs off her coat and gets to work."

"And lest we forget," Phoebe pipes in as she selects a pale taupe liner. "Taylor's porn is vanilla. He goes for the all-American thing."

"His porn?" Bridget screeches, the pencil slashing a line across her cheek.

"Oh, honey." Zach pats the sleeve of her tunic. "Okay, I'm going up to keep my eye on the sidewalk."

A few minutes later, Max claps her hands as Bridget's eyes are fixed and finalized, the liner slash quickly removed with a damp Q-tip. "Let's review deets one last time."

"Max," Zach's voice breaks into the room on speaker. "His cab is pulling up. He's alone. And he's . . . yes, he's singing to himself."

"That's my Tay."

All eyes fly to Bridget.

"Sorry, not *my*," Bridget corrects herself, embarrassed. "Just Taylor. That's Taylor. Stupid Taylor."

"Grab somebody sexy, tell 'em hey!" They can actually hear him. *"Give me eeeverything tonight, give me eeeverything tonight, give me everything . . ."*

"I'm following," Zach whispers. "Okay, it's cool— he's in."

"Remember," Max says, taking Bridget's shoulders as they huddle by the closet door. "You are the source. You are the source of the music, you are the source of the fun, you are the source."

"I am the source. Of the fun," Bridget repeats, the assertion tinged with doubt.

"Pheromone blocker," Max demands, holding her hand out like a surgeon, and Phoebe places the tincture in her palm. The slightest whiff of an ex after a period of avoidance can bombard the senses and leave a girl vulnerable. After an unfortunate incident involving Vicks VapoRub, in which a client navigated her Moment through a haze of menthol-induced tears, Max cast a wider net. She discovered this oil when mining the field of mortuary work. It dates back to the Egyptians, who created the essence to numb noses when embalming and ward off deceased spirits from poisoning theirs. *Bingo!*

"Crap, that stuff burns!" Bridget tugs back after Max dabs it under each of her nostrils.

"Just for a second, then all you smell is a hint of clove. Phoebe? Clutch." Phoebe slides the gray snakeskin Marc Jacobs from its cloth bag and hands it to Max, who gives it in turn to Bridget. Max only lends what she "borrows" to clients for their Moments. "When you beat match, start on the one, stay in the mix, ride it out, and if you juggle, get the tempos to flow."

"Get the tempos to flow," Bridget repeats. "Hey, I'm sorry I didn't tell you guys about Taylor's DJ obsession—I always thought it was so incredibly lame it didn't even seem worth mentioning."

"Let's not rehash that now—the Moment gods visited me with a bolt of genius and we're here." *Hear that, gods, I'm counting on you!*

Bridget scrunches her tissue-thin tunic. "What if no one dances?!"

Max drops her voice to a timbre that could halt a stampede. "Tonight, you are Grand Master Stetson. Okay, guys." Max huddles them, passing out the last key piece of equipment. "Earbuds in. From my position I will be able to hear and see everything, so just know—even if you can't follow what's happening, I have my eye out and this will all go smoothly."

"Testing, testing," Zach says quietly into the tiny microphone taped to his wrist. "I'm making my way to the club floor."

"Copy that," Max replies into her own, obscured by a cuff bracelet.

"Taylor is sitting at a reserved cube. The douche is in the bag."

"Zach!" Phoebe admonishes as she finishes getting ready. "So gross."

"And he's heading to the bar. You're up, kitten."

Max, Phoebe, and Bridget leave the storeroom together. Max escorts Bridget toward the DJ booth while a decked-out Phoebe splits off from them toward the bar. The DJ winds down his last song, and Bridget takes the turntables.

Despite the perspiration dampening her dress to her narrow rib cage, Bridget looks (that is, Max thinks, if anyone in the self-obsessed crowd was even looking) like she knows what she's doing. As Max snakes her way to the perfect vantage point in an alcove behind a column, Bridget puts on the first song. Max watches the floor continue to pulse and pullulate. "I can't believe this is working," Bridget whispers to her wrist.

"It is," Max intones. "Now segue into the smashup between The Kinks and The Killers."

* * *

Taylor can't believe his favorite Killers song just came on. This is a sign. Tonight is going to be A-list. No more going to parties just to end up annoyingly thinking about Bridget. He broke up with her so he could get some *living* under his belt. He's sipping his soda when suddenly a girl slips in beside him, trying to get the attention of the bartender. "Hey." She flashes him a huge smile. *Yes,* he thinks, *definitely A-list.*

"Hey," Taylor says back, his mind going blank. He realizes he never had to flirt with Bridget. He could be himself, and Bridget was always just there. Ready to laugh at his joke. Ready to ask how his day was. Then listen like she actually cared. *Dude,* enough. *No more thinking about Bridget!*

"Great DJ," the girl comments as she sways, her straw pressed between her glossy lips.

From her alcove behind a column, Max bounces her eyes between Phoebe drawing Taylor out at the long bar and the DJ booth, beyond ready for all the elements to combine, for Bridget to finally get the closure she needs. Max senses the familiar flush of triumph hovering close. It's such a delicious high seeing these girls surprise themselves with their own power in the face of their worst humiliations. She grins at being back on her game—the last few weeks really *have* just been a speed bump—

Suddenly Max sees Taylor's friend arrive and tap him on the shoulder.

Then she sees Zach and Phoebe both whip a hand to their ears as they wince from her screaming into their earpieces. "What is *he* doing here?"

"He *who*?" Zach asks.

Max forces herself to peer around the column, confirming she is not hallucinating. Nope, Cooper Baby is standing with Taylor and Phoebe, folding his leather jacket over his arm.

"It's your Tuxedo Guy from Halloween. Cool," Zach says.

"Not cool," Max says as she tries to follow the conversation on Phoebe's microphone, but it doesn't sound like Ben recognizes Phoebe without her red Black Widow wig. *Crap crap crap!* Of all the crib assemblers in the city *this* one knows Bridget's ex?! Max stares at the three of them, hoping Ben doesn't have that inexplicable instinct to whirl around and catch someone looking at him. Despite the fact that Ben is in the middle of the field, the ball is already in play.

"I'm going to the bathroom—be right back," Max

hears Ben tell Taylor. Max watches Ben turn away from the bar and maneuver around the crowd. Max's eyes widen as she realizes Ben is making a beeline for her.

Turned around by the mirrors and growing crowd, Ben circles the column—only to discover an alcove obscuring stacked crates of clean glasses. Confused, he backs up and keeps walking, unaware that the only girl in the city he really wants to see right now is shaped like a cube and trying not to breathe on the other side of the racks.

Max counts to a safe ten before springing back to her feet to see Bridget earning her first woo-hoos from the crowd. She watches Taylor lean in to hear Phoebe better when, with a well-practiced flip of the wrist, Phoebe "accidentally" douses him with tomato juice.

"Oh, I'm so sorry! Here let me help you!"

Max has to grin as Phoebe pats him down with the cocktail napkin she had concealed in her hand, spreading a dollop of olive tapenade across his chest like spackle. "Oh my God, tapenade! I'm so sorry! Where did that come from?" she asks as Taylor looks down in horror. "I'm such a klutz. It must be my new medication."

"Please, stop. It's fine." Taylor tries to back away as Phoebe ensures the mess is good and rubbed into the white cotton.

"The men's room is that way," she says, innocently pointing toward the DJ booth.

Flustered, he takes off, trying to hold his stained, wet shirt off his chest.

"Target on the move! Target incoming!" Phoebe calls into her mouthpiece, and Zach drops to his break-dance spin, the prearranged sign to Bridget. As Zach pops and locks, Bridget nods to acknowledge she's seen him and takes a deep cleansing breath, setting her intention like Max taught her.

Max watches Taylor push through the last Bebe-clad body and come face-to-face with—

"Bridget?" Max hears him ask through Bridget's wrist mike.

"Oh, hi," she says in a tone both friendly and nonchalant, keeping her eyes focused on her turntables.

Taylor's palms spread to cover up his ruined shirt. "You spin?"

"Uh-huh." She puts a finger up to pause him as she shifts songs.

"I couldn't even get you to go to a club."

"Please. You always wanted house. I'm more acid jazz. Have you heard the new Pink Shirt track?" she asks, referring to the most recent song Taylor downloaded, info she has courtesy of Zach's iTunes hacking.

"Just bought it."

She shakes her head to indicate she can't hear him, although Max knows she can. "What?!"

"I just—never mind. Wow. Well, you look . . . and the beats . . . and the . . . wow."

She holds the headphones away from her. "I'm sorry! I can't hear you!"

"You look great! Can I call you sometime?"

"Sorry! Too loud!" She smiles and shrugs, then puts her headphones back on, her tongue slipping between her teeth as she concentrates on the next track.

With a small wave, Taylor nods as he retreats backward into the crowd, getting bumped by those who are dancing with abandon to his ex-girlfriend's spin. He tries to cover for how awkward he feels, not because his shirt smells like a salad and looks like a first-grade art project, but because the girl who's been turning a dazzling focus on him since they were *doing* first-grade art projects together suddenly doesn't seem to see him anymore. And he doesn't understand why this bothers him so much.

Max throws her fist in the air as she watches a crestfallen Taylor return to the couch where his buddies stand around, nodding their heads to the beat. Taylor points to the men's room and walks away. She allows herself to look at Ben, dressed in a black button-down and narrow jeans, his hair artfully mussed. *He looks bored,* she thinks with a surprising spike of relief. She strains on the tips of her toes to see as he drops to the couch, pulling out his phone. He types something, and Max—feeling a flicker of jealousy—finds herself glancing around at the other girls nearby to see if he's writing to someone he chatted up while she was focused on Bridget. He stares down for a long moment before hitting the screen. The phone in Max's pocket dings.

"Bear misses you. P.S. Making me write this. P.P.S. Very bad breath."

Max smiles and types back without letting herself think about it. "Bear should partake of baby toothbrush." She looks back after sending the text and watches with satisfaction when Ben laughs as he reads his phone.

Her phone pings again. "Bear has strong opinions about hygiene—can't be reasoned with."

"Only because Bear does not know joys of bubble bath." Max hits SEND and watches. Ben grins and then lifts an eyebrow. He twists his mouth and types quickly. He looks around for a minute, and then two. *Hit SEND,* Max thinks. *Send to me.* Ben bites his lips and presses the phone.

Ping. "You should teach him."

Max stares at her glowing screen as the music throbs around her. She looks over at Ben. She realizes her heart has sped up. That this boy makes her heart speed up.

"Max?" Phoebe asks in her ear, and Max realizes she has inched out from behind the column. "Bridget's set is ending. You coming down to see her off?"

"Yes, yes I am."

"Oh my God!" Bridget throws her arms around Max as she bursts into the storeroom, where Max is waiting with an open Gatorade for her. "You're a genius! I mean, you described it and described it and outlined it and gave me the play-by-play, but it wasn't until I was standing there and he looked so dejected and I felt so . . ."

"Cool," Zach finishes her thought as he comes in behind her and closes the door. "You were. And now you see he's so . . ." Zach prompts for the inevitable Phase Two of The Moment. Where the shit-colored glasses of rejection are lifted and the client sees her ex clearly, remembering finally that he had pepperoni breath, was a dick to her friends, or merely hated *The Hunger Games*. She is Over Him.

"So?" Bridget repeats, seemingly not sure where Zach's going with this.

OVER YOU   155

"Lame, egotistical, short?" he offers up some popular suggestions.

"Oh." Bridget tilts her head to the side, replaying The Moment. "No. I just felt sad for him."

"He didn't suddenly look different to you? Less celebrity, more real person?"

Bridget shrugs. "He's still just my goofball Taylor. Sorry!" She slaps her forehead. "Not *my*!"

"Anyway," Zach resumes, "I vow he will speak of you, Bridget, with nothing but reverence till his dying breath."

Bridget passes back the empty Gatorade bottle. "When he dumped me, I cried so hard I—"

"Accidentally snotted on his shirt," the three finish the sentence for her.

"Projectile-snotted. I thought I was going to have to move to Guatemala and change my name to Bernice."

"And now," Max says, "you're the feather in his cap—the coolest thing he will *ever* get close to and he knows it."

The door to the storeroom opens, and Shannon and Lindsay burst in, squealing. "Okay, you crazy kids." Zach corrals them. "A town car is waiting for you upstairs. Time to celebrate at Stanton Social. A table is reserved for your dining pleasure under Max's name, and then the car will take you all home."

Bridget grabs Max's hand. "Seriously, I can't thank you enough."

"My total pleasure. And we'll see you tomorrow after school for your Closeout. Okay?" Which is always done in Max's apartment, rather than some magical Manhattan spot. In Max's mind this is like the moment the Wizard of Oz presents the long-awaited heart to the Tin Man, and it turns out to be a simple clock on a chain, the very accessibility of it making it powerful. After the VIP treatment, Max concludes the program with a basic treat—her favorite local cupcakes and a glass of milk. In ending with something clients can always do for themselves, Max underscores that the answer was inside them to begin with and therefore can't be taken away on the next guy's whim.

Bridget nods before heading into the celebratory night she has so richly earned.

"So what up?" Zach asks as Max collapses on a carton of Jim Beam, twisting open her own Gatorade. "I may be permanently deaf in my left ear."

"Sorry. Sorry. I've never known anyone in an ex's circle before—I thought that was going to blow it."

"Max," Zach says with a knowing smile. "Bridget's done, and that guy up there—"

"Ben."

"Is adorable."

"Well, that's a big, fat whatever. I'll catch him the next time my mom sends me out for onesies," she says, not ready to discuss if Ben is adorable or not. Something about Bridget's Moment is niggling at her. "Listen, can you guys pack this stuff up without me?"

"Of course."

"I just need to get some fresh air—I think I'm getting whatever the Axe equivalent of Legionnaires' disease is. I'll meet you on the sidewalk."

"Will you buy me a pretzel while you're out there?" Zach asks, unplugging the curling iron.

"Totally." She grabs her jacket, but pauses, turning in the doorway. "And you see that I can totally get this job done? That, minus some regrettable screeching, I'm totally fine? A professional you can count on? A leader you want leading?"

"Go!" Zach points out the door.

"Going!" Max makes her way to the stairs, tugging the pins from her hair. She rounds the last step to a club at full throttle. The bass moves through the soles of her heels and into her hips. And after the week she's had, she really wants to dance. Why not with Ben? Why not? A quick dance while Zach and Phoebe pack up. His bear

wants her to teach him about bubble baths. . . . She maybe
wants to teach his bear about bubble baths. . . .

The only way to reach Ben is to cut across the packed
dance floor. She begins to force her way through. Max
tries to catch Ben's eye, but he's obscured by the masses
of hair extensions and waving arms. She is about to make
it to him when she's suddenly staring directly into the
clavicle—and then face—of Hugo Tillman. His scent,
amped by the density of the crowd, almost takes out her
knees. She feels her lower jaw drop. She should say something, do something—he is all of a few inches from her.
"Hu—"

His eyes, and only his eyes, register his recognition,
and then with clear deliberation, he turns away from her
with a flat expression and pushes in the opposite direction into the crowd.

It feels like the music has stopped, and a spotlight
has whipped across the floor to illuminate her, and she
is naked and not in a good way. That did not just happen. But it did. *Jesus, Max, CLOSE YOUR MOUTH!
CLOSE YOUR MOUTH!* She struggles to retain her
balance on her thin heels as a drunken guy dances into
her. She turns, pushes, shoves, and elbows her way
out until she reaches the stairs to the exit. She tries to
walk calmly, but she's pretty sure she is running up the
main staircase. Yup, nothing graceful about how she is

gripping the railing and pulling herself up the steps three at a time.

She stumbles onto the street, past the bouncer and the waiting clubbers, hugging her bare arms across her chest pointlessly against the cold.

CHAPTER 11

M ax is not thinking anything concrete, any words or phrases that she can nail down. She's not even sure how long she's been sitting here in the dark. It must be very late, or very early, because cars don't seem to be passing outside her window anymore. The sound of the carriage clock ticking from her bookshelf . . . the orange glow of the power strip light from under her desk . . . it all feels like sensory information is traveling a great distance to reach her. Somehow she got home, unlocked her door. Her keys are right here on the floor. And now she sits on the edge of her chaise, hands on her knees, back straight. It feels like a vehicle has just hit her. But like, just. Like those movies where the actor looks sideways with a dumbfounded expression, and then the screen shows the truck or train or whatever's speeding toward him and then—*bam*. Max is at point of contact, right before the slow-motion impact sends her body flying.

That *look on his face*. That *nothing*. Even more scorching, the obvious decision he made to *do* nothing. She darts her gaze around every surface in the dim light— her desk, her dresser, her bed. Where to go? What to do to dodge the hit? If she could just hold her breath and keep from feeling this, from letting it land. She can't bear to move and begin the next second because it means acknowledging that this one has happened. She makes herself stand up, still in her coat, one hand pulling at the other. She should eat chocolate, take a Valerian, blast Pink. But instead she is walking to the stairs, as she secretly knew she might someday. Her fingers are fumbling for the switch on a nearby lamp. She is lifting up the board, taking out the box, and sinking to the floor to devour the memories she has denied herself for months. Max knows that looking at these pictures is the gateway, that within minutes of pulling out her Hugo mementos she will be listening to their songs. This will lead to full-on sobbing. But she doesn't care. She's raw and helpless from this fresh rejection. Without a card on her wrist with a number to call, the trajectory is inevitable.

The following day, just after lunch, Ben opens his school's second-floor bathroom door. "Tay?" he calls, moving down the stalls. No feet. He's about to leave when he hears a moan from under the row of stainless-steel sinks. Ben crouches to find Taylor lying on his back on the linoleum, a bloody paper towel clutched to his nose. "Someone hit you?" he asks. Taylor shakes his head. "Then why you ditching English?"

"My nose bleeds when I'm—" He cuts off.

"When you're what?" Ben asks. "Dude, Mr. Gamble is looking for you." Ben takes advantage of being out of view of teachers to scroll his phone, looking for a text from Max. Still no word from her since their bear-based exchange last night. Before Taylor flipped out and jetted. And then that girl he recognized from Model UN cornered him. "I said you had food poisoning from the sloppy joes."

Taylor maneuvers out from under the sinks with the towel still pressed to his face, obliviously continuing his own train of thought. "Since, like, forever if I get—upset," he chokes out as he stands to lean against the Formica. "My nose bleeds." His eyes glaze over. "One time Bridget and I were running a lemonade stand in, like, second or third grade. It was summer, like, gross sticky hot, she was wearing a dress . . . and I made wrong change and totally gave this guy all our earnings and Bridget—"

"Laughed at your retarded ass?"

"She was sweet about it, and blood just came gushing out my nose, and I had to run home. I didn't talk to her for, like, months after that. Why? Why'd I do that, man?" Taylor shakes his free hand at the fluorescents.

"Should I call someone?" Ben steps back, sensing he's out of his depth here. "Like, your mom or something?"

"She looked mad hot last night. Hell was I thinking?"

"What *were* you thinking?" He still isn't totally clear why Taylor decided Bridget, who had always seemed pretty cool as far as Ben was concerned, suddenly had to go. "You were so into her."

"I'm not doing the long-distance thing in college— seemed better to cut it off." Taylor groans at his stupidity. "Now it just sounds—"

"Yeah," Ben concurs. Knowing desperate times call for desperate, totally-screwing-yourself-over measures, he offers, "Listen, let's get you cleaned up, back to class, and tonight we'll go out and get your mind off Bridget."

"Thought you had to work."

"I can take one more night off." Besides, the draft Max helped him with was finally coming along.

Taylor nods unconvincingly, dropping the towel to reveal his smeared face. "Or I might hang at home and just—"

"Just what?" Ben asks, wetting another paper towel and passing it to him.

"I mean, my mom's making soup."

"We've been robbed!" Zach gasps as he steps inside Max's studio that afternoon to discover Phoebe standing over Max's prone figure on the floor. Max's head is propped on Hugo's old rugby shirt, and her coat is serving as a blanket. "Max? Oh my God." Zach steps through the scattered pictures, registering first Hugo's face in the photos and then the somber, wistful music blasting. "Is that Beck's 'Lost Cause'?"

Max pulls the coat over her face and nods before letting out a whimper.

"She's crashed," Max hears Phoebe whisper. "Our Max has crashed." Phoebe reaches down and lifts up the corner of the coat to reveal Max's eyeliner-streaked ghostly pale cheeks. "I knew it was weird when she left without us."

"We're going to have to call Bridget." Zach shakes his head. "Reschedule her Closeout."

"Zach!" Phoebe gasps. "Reschedule?"

He circles a palm at the scene. "She's still in last night's dress and heels for God's sake."

"Okay, no." Moving into action, Phoebe drops her backpack and steps over Max to the computer to mute the airy wailing—

"Leave it!" Max moans, her mouth muffled beneath the black wool.

Phoebe leaves the music on, but at a slightly less kill-yourself decibel. "Zach, grab her arm, let's get her in the shower." Phoebe lifts Max's hand but it's dead weight. "What happened, Max?" Phoebe crouches. Max pulls the coat back up and shakes aggressively from side to side.

"You're wasting your time. She's not going to tell us. Believe me—I've tried," Zach says, and even in her stupor, Max registers his hurt. "We're going to have to go CSI on this mess." He picks up a picture of Max and Hugo in their Harry Potter costumes under the eaves of a St. Something's dormitory. "And it's gonna get ugly."

An hour later, Zach hops down from where he's been hanging a makeshift piñata for Max, improvised from a stuffed bunny pilfered from the baby's room, its whiskers peeking out from behind a taped-on photo of Hugo. "It's a little over the bed, but that's the only beam I'd trust."

Phoebe flashes a thumbs-up from where she continues setting up the graduation spread for Bridget. It wasn't easy, but they managed to wrestle Max into the shower and get her to put on her yoga pants and a Splendid tee. They forced her to keep her eyes open through a speed round of the slide show, chanted some mantras at her, and are now staying on this accelerated track to get her to access some anger. Max stares at all this with hollow eyes as she leans against her dresser. But she is vertical and that, in and of itself, is an epic accomplishment. That and silencing Beck.

That evening Ben looks across the Bradleys' kitchen table at Taylor's pile of wadded, bloody Kleenex, not sure what to make of it. "Thanks for the soup, Mrs. Bradley," he says as he folds his napkin and waits for Taylor to excuse them from dinner. He takes advantage of all eyes on Daisy recounting the horrors of the afternoon's ballet misadventure to check his phone under the table. For the billionth time.

Did his last text not go through? Is Max just really busy?

Or did he totally blow it with the bubble bath thing? Did he read something that wasn't there?

After dinner they head up to Taylor's room, where Taylor immediately sinks into his desk chair and turns the volume all the way up on his computer, drowning out Ben's distracting questions about doing stuff.

"Good-bye my lover," Taylor sings along, his cheek resting on his desk. *"You have been the one for me."*

"No." Ben hits the keyboard, James Blunt still hanging in the air like cartoon squiggles over a garbage can. "I think the bro code says I'm actually obligated to shoot you in the face right now."

"You don't get it!" Taylor pushes himself to stand, spins, and falls back on his bed. "You want to watch *Star Wars?*" He reaches to fumble for the drawer he keeps his sweatpants in. "I can't go out. You want some pizza?"

"We just ate."

"I feel like pizza and Boba Fett," Taylor says as he pulls out a raggedy pair of his dad's Kenyon sweatpants. "Just stay through the gold bikini, bro. Come on. Yo, Mom!" Taylor stretches to push open his door and shout downstairs, "Make us some magic bars? Mommy?"

"And that would be my cue." Ben stands as Taylor puts in the DVD. "Call me if your brain comes out your nose again, but I gotta bounce. I have so much work that I'm having this recurring dream that I'm middle-aged and balding and still haven't finished my history paper. Like I'm still working on it at my grown-up job." He scoops up his backpack and walks out the door.

"Hey."

Ben spins back and leans through the door. "Yeah?"

"In your dream—what was your grown-up job?"

Ben's eyes glaze over at the yellow words scrolling up the black screen before tapping the door frame with his knuckles. "I don't remember. Weird." It strikes Ben that if he's ever going to figure that out he needs to stop focusing on what he doesn't want and maybe start thinking about what he does. "Later."

As the minutes tick down to Bridget's Closeout, it's as if Angelina had quit and Mary Poppins was now being played by Moaning Myrtle. Max shuffles behind Zach as he darts around her office floor trying to eradicate all evidence of Max's grief binge. She woefully drags her umbrella (makeshift bat) as he tries to set out the milk and cupcakes to toast Bridget's victory. "But *why* that look on Hugo's face?" Max asks Zach. Again.

"Are you going to want the vanilla or the chocolate— or I'm guessing you do not have a preference," he says as he arranges the celebratory confections on the plate.

"The—the nothing," Max sputters. "Like a Mr. Potato Head with all the features ripped out. Like a blank muppet. Just—nothing."

"It sounds like stoicism," Phoebe offers, rolling the linen napkins Max made from a vintage tablecloth and sliding them into their tortoiseshell holders (repurposed shower curtain rings).

"Really?" Max asks, lunging, panther-like, across the rug to her.

"Definitely." Phoebe's eyes dart apologetically to Zach. They'd been set on not indulging her, but after two straight hours of requests for analysis, Max was wearing her down.

"Zach? What did you think? Was it really a blue-blood stiff-upper-lip kind of thing? Was he dying on the inside? Was he all *Bridges of Madison County* meets *Stella Dallas* and I missed it?"

Zach places the plate carefully on the crate, which has been covered in the rest of the tablecloth for the occasion, licks the lavender frosting off the edge of his thumb, puckers his lips, and raises his eyebrows. "I do not know. I do not know if it was desperate door handle or brave Central Park rain-bonnet because *I did not see it.* It takes longer to split an atom than for Hugo to give you this nothing look you are fixated on."

"It happened," Max says woefully, looking for a spot to curl back into a ball. "The nothing look happened. I know the nothing look. I train people in the nothing look. You have your Moment, you look back, you can't help but give him a nothing look."

Zach steps between her and the chaise, crossing the arms of his tartan blazer. "Maybe he didn't see you."

"He saw me." She skirts around him, heading for her bed.

"Maybe he didn't recognize you." Zach motions for Phoebe to block her.

"He recognized me."

"Then maybe you're right—he didn't care."

"Hunhn." Phoebe and Max's collective gasp has an almost Buddhist resonance.

"That is a terrible thing to say." Max spins on him.

"Do you want to punch me?"

"Kind of, yes." Max narrows her eyes. Zach swipes up the abandoned umbrella and tosses it to Phoebe.

"Hugo Tillman doesn't care!" Phoebe repeats, placing the umbrella in Max's quivering hand.

Max lets out a wail and raises her umbrella at the bunny.

An hour later, Zach leads Bridget to the chaise.

"Doo-doo-doo!" Phoebe plays the trumpet on her fist. "Hear ye, hear ye, we now declare you, Bridget Stetson, Officially Over One Taylor Bradley." She holds up the Polaroid camera and snaps a picture of her radiance to affix to the diploma beside the original one of abject despair.

"Congratulations!" Phoebe gives her a hug. Behind

the thin screen, Max's sniffles are burbling back up to crying.

"What's that?" Bridget asks suspiciously over Phoebe's shoulder.

"Nothing," Zach dismisses, releasing her to sit on the chaise. "Just, you know, mice."

"That doesn't sound like mice," Bridget says as she cranes to look around him.

Phoebe presses her lips together. "Max is a little under the weather."

"You are seriously freaking me out." Bridget pulls her bag onto her lap like a shield. Max lets out a full sob and flops back, sending the screen toppling. Bridget leaps up as it clatters to the floor, revealing her guru, keening as a tattered bunny swings overhead. "Is this . . . stuffing?" Bridget bends to pick up a piece of cotton.

"You've got to tell us already," Zach says, helping Max up to sit on her bed.

"No," Max protests. "You'll lose all your confidence in me." She reaches for the tissue box on her nightstand and, realizing it's empty, grabs an errant tank top and wipes her nose on it.

"Pshaw." Phoebe waves a dismissing hand.

"Yes, you're the picture of confidence." Zach tugs the tank away and hands her a napkin. "Now I'm asking you as one professional to another. We obviously can't move forward if you don't just tell us exactly what Hugo Tillman did to you."

"Zachary!" Max points remonstratively at Bridget.

"Sister girl." Zach looks at Max disbelievingly before gesturing to Bridget. "This young lady here has bravely trusted us with her innermost thoughts. And I'm sorry, she's already witnessing your bottom. At least I hope this is your bottom."

"It's actually comforting," Bridget admits, reaching for a cupcake. "To know we all snot. So who's Hugo Tillman?"

"Max's ex," Phoebe explains. "Although, honestly, that's about all we know."

"Her Kryptonite. Her holy water," Zach adds.

"Her garlic." Bridget nods. "Spill it."

Max looks at the three expectant faces, knowing she's finally been cornered. "His name isn't Hugo Tillman." Max starts with a statement of fact, easing her way into the story. "Hugo Tillman lived a few hundred years ago and founded Boston. My Hugo is the Tenth. My Hugo likes argyle and rugby—the game, not the fashion line—and blueberry pie and Martin Scorsese. He smells like the European cologne his mother sends him." Collectively everyone gets comfortable in their seats as the memories overtake Max. "I was at boarding school—emphasis on *bored*. If you'd held those girls' faces to

Funny or Die, they still couldn't have made a ha-ha and for the first time in my life I was lonely. Really lonely." She looks down at her hands as she thinks how vulnerable she was to any attention. "He came looking for some girl. He noticed my red boots." She blushes as she remembers eventually standing before him in only those boots. "For five months we were inseparable." Her eyes glaze over as hundreds of memories wash over her. "He wanted me to sit with him breakfast, lunch, and dinner. If we passed in the halls he'd pull me into an empty classroom to hook up before the bell rang. Once I was studying in the library really late and I got up to find a book—I came back to my table and he'd left a bag of M&M's for me Post-it-ed with a heart."

"Oh, *that's* what this is," Zach says, raising his foot to show where it got stuck to his sole in the Hugo blizzard.

"Wouldn't you have kept it?" Max asks desperately.

"Go on."

"He said he loved me. And he introduced me to his family. I mean, how thinking-about-the-future is that?"

"So future," Bridget agrees.

"And I don't really have a family, not like that, so it was kind of like crack." She looks up at the riveted faces. "Then he invited me to be his date for New Year's Eve at their Cape Cod estate. I bought a dress. I told my mom a lie. I had it all planned out."

"What happened?" Phoebe asks.

"He was playing the final match of the season, the championship game. I was sitting in the sports pavilion, away from the rah-rah, but where I had a good view of the field. I'd dragged one of the wingback chairs over to the window. They must not have seen me there—"

"Who?"

"Elizabeth Dow Pendergast and her friends." Max can barely bring herself to say the name out loud. "They wanted to get out of the rain—their fleeces were getting damp. I heard them come in to watch. I should have said something—stuck my hand out and waved. But I didn't. They started talking about the New Year's party at Hugo's house, describing their boring dresses, their grandmothers' jewelry—and I got so excited, imagining their faces when they saw me on his arm in my backless H&M Cavalli. Then Elizabeth said Hugo. Said Hugo the same way it sounded in my head. Proprietary. I couldn't even make out the rest of what she was saying yet, it just felt like the icy drizzle on the windows was running under my skin."

"What did she say?" Bridget asks.

"'Max doesn't know about Hugo and me yet, poor thing,'" Max says, imitating Elizabeth. "Then her friend goes, 'Elizabeth, you're so patient, I don't know *how* you stand it.' And she says, 'Well, he *promised* to dump her before the party. He said he's wanted to for *ages*.'"

Phoebe and Bridget grab each other's hands.

"Oh, M," Zach murmurs in sympathy.

"That's so messed up!" Bridget exclaims.

"I can still hear the sound of the chair hitting the ground as I leapt up, but I don't remember doing it. I just remember seeing the door handle, needing to get out of there—then seeing him off in the distance. Running in the rain across the slick field. Without cleats, it was like skating. People were laughing at me. The ref was blowing the whistle. But I couldn't stop. I slammed my hands into his chest. 'You want to dump me?' I screamed. He tried to step back, he was mortified. Not by himself—by me. He was ashamed of me. I lunged forward again, but I slipped—the grass was covered in goose shit. And down I went."

The room is silent.

"That is so much worse than snotting," Bridget whispers, awed. "You lived to tell the tale and did not just move to another country to take up knitting."

"He never even said a word—"

"And was that the last time you saw him?" Phoebe asks.

"Because you dropped out at Christmas." Zach does the math.

"Right." Max nods slowly.

"You just held your head up high and walked right out of that blowhole," Zach confirms.

"Yes," Max says as she runs her palms down her thighs, her exhausted brain debating saying more. She takes a deep breath, stands on unsteady legs, walks herself to the front window, and lifts it.

"But, oh my God, if that's the last time you ever saw him—" Phoebe waves her palms at her chest in excitement.

"Yes . . ." Max says, somewhere between a statement and a question.

"Um, hello!" Phoebe jumps up. "That means there's a solution!"

"What?" Zach asks.

"Max needs her Moment!"

"Oh, snap, she's right!" Zach jumps up.

"Wait, you didn't you have your Moment, Max?" Bridget asks, the confusion returning. "But you invented it, right?"

"I did. But, actually, not until after." The cold air washing over her, Max turns to them as if seeing them all for the first time. "What do I do?"

Zach claps. "Phoebe, rolling white board! Bridget, you in or you out?"

"Oh." Bridget wipes off her hands. "So in."

"Great. Get us some cookies, markers, Kleenex, water,

stress balls, corn chips, power cords, take-out menus, and grid paper." Zach whips off his blazer and rolls up his sleeves. "Ladies, the time has come! Everything this company believes in, has been striving for and building, hangs in the balance if we can't get Max, of all people, over Hugo Snottybottom the Eight Hundredth." He strides to her and spins her around for a dip before lifting her back into a hug. "We are making a Moment! Not just *a* Moment—*The* Moment! The Moment to end all Moments! Let's make someone regret his entire existence!"

Just around this time, Ben is walking under the street-lamps of Max's block, second-guessing his half-baked plan to deliver a baby present and say he must have dropped the card. What seemed plausible a few minutes ago now just seems borderline stalkerish. He has become a crazy guy carrying a bunny blanket down the street to get a teenage girl to open her door.

He just wants to see her face, see if she's mad at him for texting un-friendly things. Or maybe she's gotten a boyfriend since they hung out. Why didn't he just kiss her?

He pauses one stoop down from hers, willing his feet to turn around—let it go. She'll text him back. Or she won't—and it was finished before it began. Then he hears her laughter. And other people join in. She's having a party? He walks closer and that's when he sees in the slice of room visible through the parted curtains, Max with her hair loose, burying her face in the shoulder of some guy with his back to the window—just like she had with him. He makes himself stand there long enough to see Max step back with her palms going to cup the guy's cheeks, her expression one of unmitigated gratitude. *Great,* Ben thinks with a sinking heart, *I missed my moment.*

CHAPTER 12

A week later, thanks to the support of Zach, Phoebe, and Bridget, Max is starting to feel like her not-sobbing-in-a-heap self again. She realizes this while walking through the corner deli on Thanksgiving morning, her arms laden with last-minute items her mother forgot, when it occurs to Max that the entire candy display isn't calling to be inhaled. Glad to no longer be craving an IV hookup to fried chocolate, she turns the aisle—and practically walks into Ben.

"Hey!" Max exclaims, her smile returning. She runs a smoothing hand down her hair, quickly trying to remember if she brushed her teeth after breakfast, or even looked in a mirror before leaving the house. "Wow, how are you? I haven't seen you in fo-ev-ah."

"Hey, uh, fine." Expressionless, Ben keeps his chin locked on the canister of bread crumbs balanced on a quart of heavy cream atop the carton of eggs in his arms.

"Last-minute stuffing crisis?" Max lifts her own buttermilk and eggs. "Where'd you find the bread crumbs?"

"Third aisle. By the cereal," he says, but makes no move to go with her.

"Cereal? That totally goes against standard grocery store code. Bread crumbs go with bread."

"It's a deli, so . . ." He stares past her.

"Right." She nods, thinking he's being weird. "How's work?"

"Busy."

"Oh."

"And you've been busy, too, right?" he says, his voice tinged with accusation before he seems to hear himself. "I mean, I hope things are cool and whatever."

"Of course." Then it hits her. He sent the last text— she was on her way to say hi at the club when Hugo derailed her—and she never followed up, left him hanging. Shit.

"Well, I have to get these home," he says.

"Hey, look, about the other night—" She scrambles, not sure what to say. "I was going to text you back—"

"But you got a better offer. It's cool."

"No," she says, surprised. But he's already moving past her. "Okay, later, I guess." Max watches him walk to the register without a glance back and then makes herself continue on to the cereal aisle. WTF? Okay, no, it's good this happened. Seriously, how well does she really know Ben Cooper? Maybe he's *not* the guy who gives great banter and looks adorable in a tux, maybe he's really the guy who gets totally pissy the first time she a tiny bit blows it, in which case, way better to know that now, before anything happened, before bubble baths. Here's what she doesn't need: another guy with the capacity to make her feel like she's sitting in goose shit.

She scans the colorful boxes until she sees the canister she's in search of and then finds herself just standing there. Or maybe he's this really great guy who put himself out there and didn't get a response and is now legitimately pissed. Guys are so confusing! She looks over at the pile of bananas. It's so clear which fruit are good and which ones are rotten. You can see it before you make your investment. Why can't boys be more like bananas? Why do you have to put your heart out there before you find out you picked a bad one?

* * *

A couple hours later the stuffed bird is almost ready for the oven and Zach and Phoebe circle the chaise with their phones clamped to their ears. "Thanks for notifying us, your friend is in good hands." Zach hangs up as Max peels chestnuts for the soup her mom will be serving Peter's family upstairs at three o'clock. "Max, can you swing an Hour One with a new client? A guy asked her *and* another girl—let's call her his backup soul mate—to the fall formal last night, ran back and forth until they both put it together when they saw *two* commemorative photo mugs drying."

Max leans over to check the time on her computer. "Yeah, but it's gonna be tight."

Zach points at the newspaper on Max's desk. "What about having your Moment on the floor of the New York Stock Exchange?"

Max shakes her head.

"Please hold." Phoebe puts her hand over her cell to whisper, "I need Max at one. And I think Max should get an internship with the architect who's designing the new Tillman building."

Max considers as she rushes through the last few chestnuts. "Round glasses, a short, wool crepe skirt—thin corduroy blazer—it has potential. But then how would I show him I'm cool with him having a girlfriend?"

"Guys!" Max's mom calls down the stairs, sending the Ex, Inc. staff into a scramble to cover notes and schedules with splayed cookbooks. Luckily Anne's voice precedes her by a few anticlimactic beats while she navigates the last steps. She's wearing yellow lattice oven mitts, which match her straining apron—one of many wedding presents she's inaugurating today. "It's nice of your friends to come over and help you cook. I told Max I could do it—"

"But you can't," Max says, finishing her sentence and tossing the last chestnut down on her desk. "Okay! Almost done with the chestnuts—next dish to prep?"

"Even *I* can follow a recipe once a year." Anne hands her the sweet potatoes to peel. "NPR's doing a piece on how this weekend is the penultimate college push. You haven't shown me word one of your essays yet, and we still need to pick your safeties. Let's sit down first thing tomorrow—go over everything. I—oof." She puts a hand to her protruding belly.

"You okay?" Max asks with concern.

"*Someone* doesn't like pie filling for breakfast," she says, placing her hand on her jumping bump. Max stiffens to hear the tone her mother had always previously reserved for her alone. But she guesses she better get used to it. The oven timer beeps above them. She looks at Zach and Phoebe. "If you don't come upstairs before you leave, have a great Thanksgiving with your families."

"You too!" Phoebe and Zach say as she waves good-bye and heads back up. They hear the kitchen door click shut.

"What about winning a national women's rugby match?" Zach suggests without skipping a beat as he pulls Max's schedule back out. "Very *Bend It Like Beckham*. Maybe with a little Brandi Chastain sports-bra action?"

"Rugby isn't soccer—I'm not going to make anyone regret anything with a broken nose."

Phoebe takes the sweet potatoes from Max's desk and starts peeling them with a Food Network–level of proficiency. "I can't believe your mom hasn't figured out that we're not over here every day just because we love your company—" Phoebe's head whips up. "I mean, we do, of course, love your *company* and *your* company. You know what I mean." In fact, if anything, since Max finally came clean with them about Hugo, she's sensing a bonding at Ex, Inc. that makes Max gratefully feel, for the first time since before boarding school, that she really has a crew again.

"Right back atcha." Max starts slicing the potatoes. "My mom's got it in her head that we're launching an

OVER YOU   185

internet dating service for teenagers, and I haven't dis-
abused her of the notion."

"She *is* an investigative reporter, right?" Zach asks.

Phoebe glares at him.

The bell rings. Startled, they all turn to the window
to see Bridget pounding in distress.

Max runs over to unlock the door. "This—this is not
the impression!" Borderline hysterical, Bridget pushes
past her into the room in her soaked basketball uniform. "This is not haunt-your-dreams! This is, 'Oh,
yeah, that's why I dumped Bridget! She gets rank and
disgusting when she plays! With a mustache! A protein
drink mustache!' Taylor's ruined my Moment! Stomped
on it. Pouf, gone!"

"Oh, God, what?" Max asks, lifting a grocery bag off
the chair and motioning for her to sit.

"I was ambushed. Our coach asked us, since we sucked
so hard at Monday's game, if we'd volunteer for an extra
practice this morning. Taylor was waiting for me when
we got out. At least at a game I'm flushed in context.
Now I'm just rank and—"

"Over him," Max declares forcefully.

"I mean, this took research. Only a few people knew
I'd be there."

"No, no, no," Max says, hearing the wavering in

Bridget's voice. "He's just flailing through how over him you are," she reiterates. "We told you that every guy tries to get in touch right after the Moment. Remember, it's designed to confuse him. Blast a hole right through his conviction."

"But this isn't right after. It's been a whole week. Maybe—" Bridget dares to voice a newly forming thought. "Maybe he's changed his mind. Maybe—"

"No," Zach interrupts.

"Not even," Phoebe says.

"Bridget." Max says her name firmly as she and Phoebe and Zach lock eyes, suddenly at DEFCON 1. "First of all, you *are* over him."

"Right . . ."

"Second, his ego has just taken a big blow. So he's falling back on some Hollywood moves, thinking if he just springs himself on you—"

"Was he sweaty?" Phoebe inquires urgently.

"Out of breath?" Zach follows up.

"It's Thanksgiving break," Max states the obvious. "He's stuck at home with his family, bored, can't jerk off 'cause the cousins keep running in and out, so he puts on his sneakers and jogs a few blocks. It's the ultimate sign that your Moment succeeded. Why deal with himself when he can call you? And why call when showing up improves his odds of—"

"Getting some," Phoebe says as Zach offers Bridget a glass of water and a damp paper towel for her green mustache.

"Getting you back," Max expands the point. "*But*"— Max holds a finger in the air— "back for all of two, maybe three hours before he turns once again into a rotting, commitment-phobic pumpkin. So he shows up when he heard you have practice, doubling his odds because his knee-jerk action has all the appearances of a grand gesture."

"Sounds like a grand gesture, in the absence of any previous thoughtfulness, even feels like a grand gesture," Zach adds as he pulls the top off a tin of turkey-shaped butter cookies.

"But it's just a big, fat half ass in disguise!" Max declares passionately. "That will shred your fresh muscles to tatters as one show-up leads to a late-night call, leads to a later-night text, leads to a lobby hookup, ending in you standing on the curb in the rain screaming for him to love you as he walks off to meet his real date. Go home. Shower. And then ask your grandmother to tell you about her coupon system and don't look at your phone until she's done. Just get through today. You have seared your awesomeness in a brand that doesn't wash off from a little sweat."

"Seriously, it's even vomit proof, we've tested," Phoebe adds.

"And no matter what, Bridget," Max says as she escorts her toward the door. "No matter how, you do not do anything but smile and keep walking, are we clear?"

"This is a slippery slope," Zach adds over a passing fire engine's alarm.

"A dark, humiliating, ripped-stocking-and-broken-heels-in-a-rainstorm slope," Max confirms, her face darkening. "No one has ever come back from getting rejected by the same guy twice. *No one.*"

"Twice?" Bridget asks in horror.

"Angie. Riverdale," all three say in unison.

"Finished the program," Zach explains.

"Rocked the program," Phoebe adds with a nod from Max, who has drilled this cautionary tale into them. "Then," Phoebe continues, "her ex left a love letter in her locker."

"Which, I might add, was typed," Max tosses in.

"And she wouldn't listen to Max." Phoebe puts a hand on Bridget's arm.

"Max pleaded," Zach says.

"And pleaded," Phoebe echoes.

"What happened?" Bridget asks, looking scared.

"It got ugly," Max says like a weathered war reporter.

"There were love songs played outside windows, there was a late-night visit in *just* a coat—that blew open in front of the garbage man. There was begging. And then . . ." Max quickly finishes the story, eager to move them along. "She followed him to college, where he got a restraining order against her. Look, this isn't about Angie, it's about you."

"But—"

"No buts, Bridget."

"Turkey cookie?" Zach offers.

"Ew," Bridget responds succinctly.

"Turkey-shaped," Zach corrects himself.

Bridget takes one. "Okay. Angie Riverdale. I get it," she says, not sounding entirely convinced. "I trust you." She eats her cookie pensively as Max picks her knife back up. "So how is your Moment coming, Max?"

"Well, unless I can find a unicorn to vanquish on the floor of the New York Stock Exchange while I design a sports arena in which I win the World Cup topless—it's not. I'm about as tranquil as a Missoni dress."

Zach takes a cookie and bites off its frosted, wattled head—his eyes suddenly going as wide as Max's.

"What?" Phoebe and Bridget ask.

"Missoni!" Zach and Max raise their hands toward each other, hooking fingers. "Missoni!"

"Can you fill the rest of us in?" Phoebe asks.

"It could be perfect," Zach marvels.

"Perfect. But can we?" Max asks him as the logistical challenges of sneaking Max into *Teen Vogue*'s benefit for the upcoming Missoni exhibit at the Met unspool before her.

"I don't know—can we?"

"What?!" Phoebe and Bridget cry.

Max and Zach nod at each other, ready to drive off the cliff rather than give up. "Okay, ladies, get your Tom Cruise on," Zach exhorts. "We're going Moment: Impossible!"

The following night, the brunette from Model UN, the one Ben ran into at the Cabin, is talking to him. She has broken away from the clique of girls huddled in the corner of his friend Vance's (short for Vancouver, city of his conception) living room. Vance's parents are spending Thanksgiving weekend at their ski house, having left their son behind to get a jump on his college applications, unknowingly freeing Vance to hold court over a game of beer pong in their kitchen. Those not beer ponging are gathered around the living room's flat-screen in a virtual ultimate fighting championship that predominantly entails slouching into the L-shaped couch. And leaning on the back of this couch is Ben—completely unaware that the smile he is smiling is being received on the wrong frequency by this rogue girl.

Ben is smiling because, for a brief momentary respite, he's only remembering what it felt like to hold Max against him that night at the store. He reaches for a handful of chips, and his brain flips back like a pancake that's burnt on one side. Why did she seem hurt by him yesterday at the deli if she has a boyfriend?

"So did you guys end up staying at the Cabin the other night?" The brunette tilts her ear to her shoulder and tugs at her necklace, a metallic lightning bolt pendant. "Ben?"

"No, my friend wasn't too into it."

"That Taylor guy? Doesn't he skate with Vance?"

"Yeah." Ben glances at the wedged-open front door in search of Taylor, who's over half an hour late.

The brunette grabs Ben's hand. "Oh my God, I have the exact. Same. Phone," she states with an awe appropriate to discovering she and Ben share a parent. "Wait right here. This is so crazy! I have to show you." She backs up and around the couch, eliciting a rolling wave of *"Move!"* from the gamers.

Ben drains his cup and then adds it to the cluster covering the nearby dining table. He wonders if Max is staring at a similar spread of abandoned plastic cups right now.

"Ben."

He looks up to see Taylor, hat pulled low, hands pushed deep into his vest pockets, dodging over—*"MOVE!"*— in front of the TV.

"Finally." Ben leans in for a hug, but instead of the usual, quick, two-back-pat greeting Taylor is stiff. Ben looks at him and sees that the rims of his eyes are red. Taylor's definitely been out of it this week, but this is— "You okay? You look like hell."

"I, uh, ran into Bridge."

"On your way here?"

"Yesterday morning. Dude, why didn't you answer your phone?"

"My two-year-old cousin hid it in her diaper bag. Don't ask." It was actually the least of his stresses on a day when his parents were in the same room for hours on end, his extended Italian family needing to pretend divorce doesn't happen on Thanksgiving, Christmas, and the Feast of St. Anthony. "So what happened—did she finally lose her shit on you?" Ben asks.

"Yeah, no. I mean, not like that, she—"

"See? Same. Exact. Cover." A phone is thrust between them, clutched by five black fingernails. The brunette pushes herself through the opening she's made and looks up at both boys. "I was going to go all black, too, but I thought the blue case was way prettier. So Taylor made it! This is Gwenie." She pulls her friend forward, forcing Taylor to take a step back. "I'm Kim."

Gwenie tugs at Taylor's vest. "Oh my God, aren't you so hot?" The music stops, and Gwenie's adjustment from screaming to talking happens three words too late. A few guys turn with mild interest from the couch before a driving hip-hop beat blasts the room. "This is my joint!" Gwenie shrieks and starts grinding on Kim's hip. Kim flashes Ben a grin before reciprocating.

Ben takes in the floor show while simultaneously taking in everyone else doing so. He doesn't even recognize half these kids. Some are pudgier versions of their senior selves, back from college for break, with an air of owning the place. Whatever. Okay. Yes, these two are cute. Cute enough to get his mind off Max—maybe. Kim has a brown ponytail swung over her popping shoulder that's almost the color of Max's. Do this. Stay with this. "So, uh . . . let's get out of here," Ben suggests.

"And go where?" Gwenie asks, including herself in the directive.

Ben shrugs, knowing the girls will fill it in for them.

"Ooh, let's go to Silk Road. I'm *starving*," Gwenie asserts. "We'll grab our coats. Hold on," she says dramatically as though if she didn't, the boys might race to get there first. Ben nods, and the two dart away.

"I'm not really feeling greasy Chinese and banter about your cell soul connection," Taylor says as he leans into Ben. "I'll hang for a few and then you can take this one solo."

"Dude, what happened when you ran into Bridget?"

"Okay, I didn't run into her so much as . . . look, her mom saw my dad at the market, told him Bridge was at practice—I jogged over to catch her before she left."

Ben stares at him, his face conveying the "what were you thinking?" it would feel mean to say out loud.

"I thought she'd do that little Bridget hop when she saw me—the one she used to do when I met her after school," he says defensively. "I miss watching her play— you wouldn't think it 'cause she's so little—but she's fierce on the court."

Ben doesn't know what to say.

"Being in my bedroom is like some game where I try to look everywhere but out my window. I never see her there anymore, like, her lights are never on. I needed to see her. See her do that hop." Taylor cups his hat brim. "I'm gonna bail."

"Do you want her back? I mean, you know I think she's cool."

"No way." Taylor shakes his head like this is an insane question. "I just miss her. I don't know, I thought we could be friends. But now . . . She turned and ran away, dude. Ran away."

"I'm sorry, that sucks, Tay. It really does." Ben lifts his elbow at the girls pulling on their short leather jackets by the door, not wanting to end the night staring at the Halloween pics on his phone again. "But, look, they're cute."

"They're wasted."

"BOYS, COME *ON*!" Gwenie falls back against the door frame like she's fainting. Kim fake pouts.

Denying Taylor the chance to protest, Ben follows the girls out.

"Your friend's kind of a mess," Ben says to Kim as Gwenie, yet again, stumbles into Taylor as they walk about ten yards ahead.

"Yours is kind of a downer," Kim counters with a grin. "Together they're *adorable*."

"Right." Ben laughs.

"Cute smile," Kim says, giving him a glance as they mosey along. "I remember that from Model UN."

"Thanks." Ben blushes.

"What was your thing? Uzbekistan?"

"Kurdistan. I drew it out of the teacher's briefcase." Ben shrugs.

"Do you remember mine?" She steps in front of

him, walking backward.

"Um, France?" he lies, having not a clue. "Someplace with style."

"That's funny. Uganda."

"Uganda." Ben nods. "Of course."

"Totally the same as France." She grins, her hair tilting seductively into her face under the streetlight. "So note to self: I need to be more memorable." And before Ben knows it she has placed a hand on either of his arms and stopped him with a hot kiss.

Meanwhile, forty blocks north, the elevator raises Zach and Max higher and higher inside 4 Times Square. "Nice jacket," Max comments approvingly.

"I thought—if we get busted we can just tell them we were on our way to find your mom and got lost. Harris tweed says, '*New Yorker* intern who bird-watches on the weekend.'"

"And if we get stopped in the closet?"

"This jacket also says, 'I intern at *Teen Vogue* and am looking for a royal sugar daddy to take me pheasant hunting.' It's multilingual."

Max leans back against the brushed steel. "What does it say if someone finds out I happen to have several thousand dollars' worth of clothes in my tote?"

"You're making me sweaty."

"Relax. I've done this so many times I could sleep-walk it."

The elevator bypasses her mother's offices on twenty and carries them right up to *Teen Vogue*.

"But you've never done *this*," he reminds her.

"No, I've never done *this*." And she feels the bravado she'd been carefully cultivating evaporate as the oxygen thins. "Okay," she whispers as they get off, "I'm going straight to the closet while you find a computer—"

"I can't!" He grabs her arm.

"Are you suddenly having a moral crisis on me? Higher good, Zach! Higher good!"

"Oh God, no. I'm just wondering if Anna Wintour still puts people in stocks?"

"Okay, I don't think she ever did that—come on, you're going to love it here."

She leads him along the row of desks to a computer whose screen saver is still on, meaning the computer's just asleep—not shut down—and no password will be required. Max sits Zach down, hovering over his bank-rolled bird-watching shoulder. "Okay, do your thing."

He takes a deep breath and then hits the keyboard like Schroeder tackling the piano. Suddenly he stops typing.

"What?" Max asks, peering over his shoulder. "Is it

not there—ooh, killer shoes," she says, momentarily distracted as layouts pop up alongside article proofs. Then she realizes the top headline Zach's staring at asks: IS YOUR FRIENDSHIP FOR REAL?

"I still don't understand why you couldn't just tell me," he says, pushing back from the desk.

"What?"

He turns to her. "You showed up on my doorstep last Christmas in that cute Zac Posen dress—"

"God bless Target."

"But you looked like shit."

"Hey."

"Your eyes were like empty holes. You could barely smile. But when I asked you what happened, you blew me off."

Max tenses. "Saying I wasn't ready to talk about it isn't blowing you off!"

Zach throws his hands up. "Since when don't we tell each other everything? So you slipped in shit, whatever. I thought I meant more to you than that."

Max can't bring herself to explain. "You do."

"Fine," he says, even though it's so not. But Max doesn't know how to make it fine right now.

He turns back to the computer and resumes their search.

Max looks to the clock. "We can't stay out in the open

much longer like this." He doesn't answer. "Zach," Max says desperately.

"I'm going as fast as I can!" He types while Max backseat mouse scrolls. "Okay, here, yes." He opens the folder they've been looking for: the RSVP list for the party of the year. The Costume Institute's Young Collectors' Benefit, sponsored by *Teen Vogue*.

"Wow," they say together as they scroll the guest list. Selena Gomez, Robert Pattinson, Emma Roberts, Emma Stone, Emma Watson—"Come on, come, come on," Max says as they get to the bottom of the list. "This is all for nothing if we're wrong." But then they scroll back up and see it. Hugo Tillman. "Yes!" Max pumps her fist. Plus one. "Plus one?!"

"That's the point, genius," Zach mutters.

"Right, no, of course." Max realizes if she doesn't tell Zach how things actually ended with Hugo, they may never be okay again—for real.

Zach scrolls to the Condé Nast Junior Committee list and types Max's name into the program proof.

"Here we go," Max says as Zach clicks ENTER.

A few minutes later Zach and Max are nestled deep inside the closet. "What about this?" Zach asks, spreading the racks to hold out a green, scale-patterned Oscar de la Renta number.

"Too much," Max says, taking in her reflection in chiffon Carolina Herrera, the bodice of which is composed of tastefully placed peacock feathers that pick up the flecks of green in her eyes.

"Okay, what about *this*?" He holds up a crocheted white doily.

"Too little."

"What are we going for?" he asks impatiently, seemingly over the whole undertaking.

She sighs, turning her back to the rack and leaning against the clothes, tipping in at the waist. "A part of it all. On the inside. Establishment," she says, trying to pull him back to being her wingman extraordinaire. "But I want to take his breath away. More Audrey Hepburn at the end of *Roman Holiday* than Olivia Newton-John in *Grease*." Truthfully when she tries to picture herself facing off with Hugo and his girlfriend, increasingly in her imagination the Perfect Dress blurs and the Perfect Setting blurs—and then the face that's left staring into hers is . . . Ben's. "I saw it here once: it was a simple, red column—kind of naked, but totally elegant."

"Red, red, red," Zach says, going from rack to rack. They pull everything red, but it isn't there anymore.

"Shi—" She doesn't get to finish because Zach clamps his hand over her mouth. She goes to whip it away, but then she hears it, too.

Zach shuts off the light and they dive under the nearest rack, pulling the ends of dresses over them. Max tries not to breathe—and then wonders if she even can as it sinks in that she may have just gotten her best friend arrested. Which will mean expelled. Which will mean rejected from anywhere he wants to apply next year. All of which he risked, going to the mat for her, when she couldn't even be honest with him.

"Zach," she says.

"Shhhh."

"I'm Angie Riverdale."

The door opens.

The guard's flashlight slowly passes over them. Max can feel her cheeks swell as she tries to keep from exhaling. Her heart is so loud she's sure the guy can hear it. The flashlight swings back to the rack they are behind. The beam holds steady over Max's arched back, which she hopes is blending with the black dresses dangling in front of her. Zach is staring at her, his eyes huge. The guard moves away, and the door closes.

"Let's get these feathers off me, in the bag, and let's jet." Max springs into motion.

"Whoa." Zach doesn't move. "Angie Riverdale metaphorically? Or literally?"

"Literally," she confesses. "The first time we had a client who wanted to take her ex back I started to use myself as an example—a cautionary tale—but you were both so horrified that I changed course and said it had happened to an early client. It doesn't matter." She tries to downplay the enormity of her confession. "I just, you know, if we were going to jail—"

"So Hugo typed you a love letter and you went back to him?"

"Or something." Max stares at her feet.

"You went back to him, and he didn't even have to write you a letter?"

"It was more of a note. He might just have been asking me to give his rugby shirt back. The story has evolved to . . . suit the needs of our clients."

"'Ripped stockings in a rainstorm' is an *evolution*?"

"Yes." Max takes a deep breath. "Okay, I didn't just pack up and leave St. Something's. I mean, I'd been moving for forever and then I'd never been so lonely and then Hugo loved me, gave me a place to be, really *be*, and I didn't know how to just give it up. I stayed at school for about two more weeks. I called him, showed up at his room." She drops her head. "We would hook up and then I'd ask him to look me in the eye and tell me there was nothing between him and Elizabeth and he couldn't and I'd start sobbing. His friends started calling me McCrazy. People laughed at me in the halls. It was brutal." Her mouth quivers as she remembers the cocktail of humiliation and need she was drowning in.

"But you did leave," Zach says gently as he helps her step out of the dress. "You're here, aren't you?"

"This has to be perfect, this Moment." Max clutches his shoulders to steady herself, hearing her own voice say what every client has said to her. "Because I may have tweaked the story for everybody, but I didn't tweak the point—I really don't think I can come back from this if it doesn't."

CHAPTER 13

Ben doesn't believe it, but he's actually finished the common application. He's reread his essay so many times the words stopped making sense, like it wasn't even written in English or something. Now he wants to stick it in the mail before the impulse to rip open the seal and check it one more time gets too strong to suppress.

On the last Friday afternoon before Christmas, the main post office is as packed as the subway into the city had been. The line of people waiting to ship their gifts to far-flung relatives snakes multiple times before stretching out one of the doors. *Do not rip open any of the envelopes,* Ben tells himself. *You'll be stuck here until New Year's to buy a new one.*

Ben's not surprised Taylor's late. They'd made this plan last year, late night, when a keg was tapped and they were fuzzily sentimental. They cheers-ed their plastic cups to the idea of ceremoniously mailing their Kenyon applications together to get them in ahead of the rush. They were then going to cross over to Penn Station, where they'd hop the train to Vance's annual ski weekend.

Now Kim's going to be there with some other girls. They've talked a few times and she seems cool. Yeah, he's looking forward to it, if Taylor could just hurry up and get here already.

Ben spots him trudging up the steps with his head hung like some old guy, his parka unzipped despite the flurries. Even from this distance he looks like ass, but at least his nose doesn't seem to be bleeding, so there's that!

"Sorry, do you mind holding my place?" Ben asks the old lady behind him pushing a grocery cart of packages topped with a lounging cat. "I just have to grab my friend, I'll be two secs."

Ben pushes through the glass door and jogs down to get Taylor to pick up his pace. "What's up?" Ben asks as he approaches. "You still sick?" Taylor just keeps trudg-ing. Ben waves a beckoning hand to hurry him, jogging suggestively a few steps ahead even. Taylor's oblivious. "I could have just gone to my local post office," Ben says as they reach the heavy brass doors, "and met you on the train."

"It's cool," Taylor responds unconvincingly as Ben points him to their saved place in line. Surrounded by harried, sweaty, middle-aged people and a mopey, mis-erable, potential roommate, attempting a ceremonious anything feels officially lame. Not even noticing the cat, Taylor swings his slack backpack off his shoulder and withdraws his applications.

"This line is mad long," Ben mutters as he looks into the near-empty bag, guessing Taylor does not have his ski pants in there either. As they approach the home stretch to the tellers, Ben fends off a flood of doubts about what he wrote, what he didn't write, and why spending the next four years with a guy he feels like he doesn't know anymore at a school he isn't sure why he wanted to go to in the first place seems like a good idea. Mostly what he thinks of is Max figuring out graduating early, applying to one school—and doing it all on her own. "So you traveling light?" Ben shifts his straining bag to his other shoulder.

Taylor nods listlessly.

"You going to borrow gear from Vance?"

"Vance?" Taylor looks confused.

"To ski?"

"Oh, yeah. Nah. Not up to it." Taylor shrugs.

"It's our last Ski Weekend of Debauchery."

"Yeah, have fun."

Ben snaps. "Look, Tay, I spent eight weeks busting my ass on this application. So I can get in somewhere that, at the end of the day, you're getting into even if you farted on that thing and left it blank, which, given your zombie state, I'm thinkin' you did."

"Just 'cause I'm a legacy, that's totally not true. I filled it out, Ben. I wrote my essay. Jesus, what's your problem?"

"My problem is I didn't see you for an entire sum-mer. Then you need me to go out like you're making up for your lost youth. And now you're acting like some-one cut your balls off and you're bleeding to death very slowly. Is this what school with you is going to be like?"

People are looking at them over their brown pack-ages. A weird smile spreads across Taylor's face. He waves to motion for more. "This is good!"

"What?" Ben's alarmed.

"No, it is! I need to be pushed! Nobody has—Bridget used to challenge me. Every time I wanted to make a wussy choice. This is good, yell at me."

Ben steps closer, dropping his voice. "I kinda said what I had to say."

"And you're right. Totally right. I'm walking around with Kleenex in every pocket." He withdraws his hand to display the wads. "This morning, my mom suggested I need 'a good cry.' I do not need a good cry. I need Bridget to answer my calls. Or my emails. Or my messages. Or my texts. Or my tweets." To Ben's surprise, Taylor grips him by the shoulders. "You said it. I need to man up."

"I mean about college." *And us,* Ben thinks.

"I thought I had to break up with Bridget to make college better, instead I'm just making myself and you crazy. I have mad respect for you, dude. You work your ass off." Taylor pulls Ben in for a hug, Ben's face deflating the green down puff of Taylor's coat. "You've brought me back, BC."

"I have?"

"You have. I don't want to sit around Vance's kitchen and play quarters until the sun rises. I don't want to chat up townie girls between Journey numbers at the lodge's karaoke. And next year I don't want to roam campus parties trying to find what I already had. I want my girlfriend back."

"Okay, I mean, that's great, but—"

"As soon as we mail this in, I'm setting up camp on Bridget's stoop until she'll talk to me. How can I give up if I haven't put all my cards on the table?"

"You're up," the cat woman says to them, tilting her head at the available window. Taylor strides to the teller while Ben waits, the envelopes in his hand, wishing he felt as sure about what to do next.

Max is standing in six thousand dollars' worth of illegitimately borrowed peacock feathers and her priceless, fuzzy Wisconsin cheese slippers when the doorbell rings. "Oh my God!" Max cries as she spots Ben through the window, her heart spiking in her chest like a football. She flattens against the wall. *"Music off!"* she hisses at Zach, who's testing peacock-complementing toenail colors on his own fingers.

"The S.S.?" Zach asks theatrically as he hits MUTE.

"Ben!" Max reaches to her side to find the perfectly hidden zipper that is too damn perfectly hidden.

"Maybe he'll think you're not home." Phoebe crouches at Max's ribs to aid her search.

"How could he not have heard the music?" Max finds

the tiny turquoise zipper, navigating the pins she used to baste the seam just a touch tighter. "And I want him to think I'm home! Coming!" she calls.

On the other side of the door Ben finds himself bouncing a little on his toes. *Whatever happens, I'm putting my cards on the table,* he thinks as he pep-talks himself, his ski bag between his ankles. His phone buzzes with a text from Kim.

"Looking forward to getting our delegations together. ☺" Is this crazy? Should he just have gotten on the train?

Inside Zach tugs the soda-can-sized rollers from the top of Max's head. "I told you it was a premature hour for Pink." He tsks.

"Just getting out of the shower!" she shouts to the door before spinning back to Zach. "I needed a break from listening to recordings of Hugo's voice. I'm moving from desensitized to deaf." Max steps from the dress just as Phoebe holds out her leggings to jump into like she's a toddler.

"It's not my fault," Phoebe protests. "The only thing I could find online was his yacht-club rap. I still can't believe they recorded that talent—and I use the term loosely—show."

Max tugs her peacoat on over her bare chest. "I'd

rather put lit matches in my ears than hear him say 'boa-
tin' with my boyz' one more time," she attests as she
wedges her feet back into her slippers.

"Well," Zach says, "in three hours and counting
you'll never have to hear him say anything again." And
then all that remains is Max's NYU presentation to Dr.
Schmidt—the life that was starting to feel so blurry is
regaining clarity.

Zach nods at them both to indicate he is about to open
the door.

"Ben!" Max steps onto the threshold, angling the
door behind her to obscure her two assistants diving out
of view. "Hi!"

"Can I come in?" he asks nervously.

"You know, I could use some air. I'll come out."
Max pulls the door shut, and Ben takes a step back on
the brick. He looks down at her slippers. Trying to pretend the furry, orange triangles are Louboutins, Max
walks around and up to the main stoop to get out of
Phoebe's and Zach's earshot. She takes a seat, and he sits
down beside her. She looks at Ben, waiting for him to
say whatever he came to say, but as the beats of silence
drag on, she wonders if she needs to push herself to
make the next move. "So, how've you been?" she asks
tentatively. "How's the essay coming?" A thick chunk

of hair that had been Elnetted stiff flops into her face and catches on—

"Wow, your eyelashes." Ben stares as she tries to pick the two apart. "I never noticed how long they are."

Right. Because Phoebe hasn't trimmed them yet. The Double Lush Diva length probably seems a little much when not being viewed from, you know, outer space. "Yes, this is just . . . for work."

"Are you a . . . hostess?" His voice rises with his most, let's face it, polite guess. "You never told me. But I guess you wouldn't be going to NYU for hospitality."

"No, not exactly. Long, boring story."

Ben looks at her for a minute, waiting for her to start it, thinking there could never be anything boring about her. Then he realizes she isn't going to, and he has to just *say* something. "Um, so, my best friend is having, like, a nervous breakdown, and it's gotten me thinking—"

"A nervous breakdown?" Max can't help scoff.

"Well, kind of. He's obsessed with his ex-girlfriend. He's, like, totally stalking her."

"Well, maybe he shouldn't have kicked her to the curb in the first place."

"I guess, but—wait, how did you know that?"

"What?" Max's cheeks redden. "I assumed it."

"Because he's a guy?"

Max feels her pulse picking up and not in a good way. "Because that's what guys tend to do, yeah."

"Okay, he's really a mess."

She pivots a little to face him, acutely aware of the Ex, Inc.–sized gulf she's going to have to cross if she wants to be any closer; that is, if he wants to be. She looks at his broad shoulders, the confusion in his chocolate-brown eyes. She wants to be closer. She really does. "Sorry. I'm listening."

"Look, I didn't come here to talk about Taylor. Before you say anything else, I just need to tell you that—I know you and I are friends. We were becoming friends." He looks down at his feet. "But I kind of felt like there was maybe something more . . ."

He's going to say it, Max thinks. But he should know about Ex, Inc. first—because if he finds out she's behind why Taylor's having this so-called breakdown . . . She doesn't know what to do. "Ben?"

"Yes."

"There's something I have to tell you."

"You have a boyfriend." His shoulders hunch. "I know."

"What? No! I totally do not."

"I saw a guy in your window the other night—"

"You were looking in my window?"

"I was passing by with a delivery."

Her forehead accordions in disbelief. "Look, if you saw a guy in my window at night it was either (a) my stepfather, or (b) Zach, or (c) a stalker watching me in my sleep."

"Zach?" he asks.

"Iron Man. And his boyfriend would seriously think it was weird if Zach was watching me sleep."

"Oh." A flush moves up Ben's cheekbones.

"But . . ." She flips her cheese wedges from side to side, trying to figure out the best way to begin. "Look, there's something I do that you might not . . . hmmm . . . you know when you've been dumped and—"

"Um, can't say that I have."

"You've never been dumped?" This brings her up short.

"No—"

"You've never had your heart broken?" She climbs to her feet. How could this possibly work if he doesn't get heartbreak?

"I've never gone out with anyone really seriously before," Ben says as her other curl droops.

"Wow, that's—wow." How could he even begin to understand her—what she does?

Ben can see she's thrown. "I hope that's not a deal breaker." He holds out his hand and she takes it, the feel of his palm against hers warm and sparking. She sits back down. "You can't hold that against me. I never had the opportunity—never met someone worth it."

He looks in her eyes, trying to gauge if she wants this. Her gaze is steady on his, and he leans in, his lips landing gently on hers until hers press back, reciprocating, their kiss building so quickly in intensity that it shocks them both. "You're worth it," he murmurs. "I don't want to just be friends with you, Max."

The first thing Max thinks—when Max *can* think again—is he's an incredible kisser. He wraps his arms around her, his palms spreading across her back, pulling her as close as possible as his lips move to her ear. "That's what I came to say."

"Okay," she manages.

"That's all you have to add?" he asks, his fingers trembling as they meet the bare skin under her coat. "Okay?"

"Mm–hmm," she says, forgetting that there was something she thought she had to do to make this possible when touching him feels like the simplest thing she's ever done.

He grins. "Let's have a date. Wear your cheese shoes if you want, but I made a reservation at the French place on Court Street. No cribs, no bears, no essays."

She tilts the tip of her forehead against his. "I love the French place—but tonight I have this thing I have to do for work, which I will tell you about later. But it'll be over by nine. I just have to swing by and do this thing that I need to do to do this."

"You lost me."

"The point is I will be in a dress that is the opposite of these." She kicks out a slipper. "Date with a capital *D*. Let's go out in the city. Dust off that tux, 007. I'll text you the address, and we'll hang fancy."

"As non-friends."

"Extremely," Max says as she jumps down the steps.

Taylor's sandwich is gone, his Snapple is drunk, and the December wind is blowing through his coat as he sits on Bridget's stoop. He dials his phone. After a few rings, Daisy throws open her bedroom window.

"What do you want, loser?" she yells across the street.

"A scarf, *The Scarlet Pimpernel*, and another Snapple!"

"It's not going to be much of a stakeout if you pee on yourself!" she shouts back.

"Just do it!"

She slams the window. But after a few minutes his front door opens, and she comes between the parked cars, arms full. "Snapple." She hands off the bottle. "*Pimpernel.*

A scarf. A silky." She passes him the long-sleeved T-shirt.

"Where'd you get this?" He looks at it dubiously.

"Dad's ski drawer. You're gonna freeze, Taylor."

He ruffles her hair.

"Hey, that's my ballet bun!" She recoils, smoothing her hand over the thatch of bobby pins.

"You don't have ballet today."

"I was practicing." She humphs. "Okay, call if you need anything else, but don't abuse me," she parrots their mother.

"Okay, Linda." He uses their mom's name. Daisy narrows her eyes at him and flounces back into the house. Taylor smiles to himself as he tugs off his coat and, with a quick breath, pulls off his shirt in preparation to pull on the undershirt.

His eye catches Carrie Hendricks as she rounds the corner. She tosses her hair over her shoulder and walks straight over.

"Taylor! Hey!" she says in her husky voice that sounds like she perpetually has a cold. Which should be repulsive, but isn't. Nothing about Carrie is. "Stripping?"

"Right, no, I'm . . ." *Stalking.*

"Missed you at Vance's party last weekend."

"Yeah, Ben and I bolted early." Taylor looks left and right down the block. He pulls the undershirt on. Here it is—the girl he dumped Bridget for, his moment to flirt, but he just can't seem to summon the mojo.

"Bummer. I always think of you with that crowd." She kicks the stoop with the toe of her scuffed flat, trapping his shirt and jacket. She leans down toward him, and he gets a full view of her impressive cleavage. "Should I take my coat off, too?" It slides off her shoulders to the step with his.

He whips his gaze from her boobs—to the corner—then back to her boobs—then to her eyes—his boy-brain splitting. He doesn't even hear the cab pull up.

"Taylor?!" Bridget, one foot out of the car, looks stunned. "Oh my God, you're naked!" she cries. "On my stoop! This is so much worse than ambushing me at school! Half naked with Carrie Hendricks on my stoop!"

"Bridget!" He leaps up, pulling on his coat.

"Asshole!" She slams the cab door, and he hears her say "Brooklyn."

"Bridget, wait!" He runs after the car, catching the handle, slapping the window with his other hand. The door opens, throwing him to the street.

"Stop," she screams to the driver as Taylor's body rocks to a prone position. Bridget leaps out. "Tay?"

"Okay, so you're talking to me," he croaks, looking

up at her concerned face. God, he loves that face. "This is good."

She peers at him for a moment, her expression concerned. But then she glances at Carrie.

"Please," he begs, "give me a chance here."

Instead she gives him her hand, and he sits so they're face-to-face. She bites her lip.

"Bridge," he says, "I freaked out. I shouldn't have ended it."

She nods, taking this in. "Yeah. You did," she says finally, wrapping one arm across her stomach. "But I can't undo that. I'm supposed to be over you." She stands up and gets back into the waiting cab. She shuts the door. "Drive, sir, please." Taylor can hear the tears breaking in her voice, and he hates himself, feeling really, truly, for the first time, sorry—not for himself and what he's lost, but for the pain he's caused her.

A little while later, the stars and passing planes twinkle in the indigo evening sky as Max's town car pulls up to the curb. The benefit has been set up in tents covering a full block of the High Line, the old elevated railroad tracks now converted to a park over the fashionable Meatpacking District. Photographers snap their flashes at the red-carpeted stairs leading to the tent, and stretch limos jockey for space on the cobblestones. Max is ready. From her Fire Sapphire-ringed eyes, to her Brazen Bronze blush, her Over You Look is in place. It is the epicenter of glamour, but all Max can think about is getting her Star Pink lips back beneath Ben's.

Her driver opens her car door, and she gathers up the hem of her billowing gown to jog past a few limos to where Zach and Phoebe are unloading surveillance equipment from their gypsy cab.

"How we doing in here?" She opens the back door to see Bridget hunched behind the passenger seat, still sniffing, her eyes even more red and puffy than they were thirty minutes ago when her cab pulled up just as they were leaving Brooklyn.

"She keeps going on about a Carrie Riverdale and Angie Hendricks," Zach calls around from the trunk.

"Carrie Riverdale and Angie Hendricks," Phoebe corrects as she applies her red lip gloss. "The girl stopped making sense somewhere around Chinatown."

"Why?" Bridget beseeches, clutching Max's arm—tugging her torso into the car.

"What?" Max asks, steadying herself on the seat, looking past Bridget and out the window to where the flow of celebrities is slowing to a trickle. Photographers are starting to pack up their gear as the event begins in earnest. She's got to get in there.

"Why can't I go back to Taylor?" Bridget pleads. "What if he really means it, and he really learned his lesson? What if I'm tossing aside an awesome guy who actually really loves me for Carrie Hendricks to scoop up?"

"No," Max answers firmly. "Nonononono."

Bridget releases Max and frantically grabs for the door handle. "I have to go find him! I have to!"

Max reaches over her and hits the lock. "Zach, keep her with you," she calls to where he's miking Phoebe on the sidewalk. Max turns back to Bridget, moving into *Scared Straight!* mode. "Bridget Stetson, if you go back to him I am done. You are on your own. I'm cutting you out of this program and out of my life." Max pulls back out of the car and slams the door.

"Wow," Phoebe says, lowering her gold compact mirror.

"I'm going in." Max tugs off her coat.

"Chill, girl, we haven't even miked you yet!" Zach unzips the first duffel.

"I don't need a mike. I don't need him to be tapanaded. I don't even need him to see me chatting with the CEO of Condé Nast. Scratch it all. He's just going to give me a big nothing look, and I'm going to give my nothing look back, and I'm going to walk once around the room like I belong there. Then I'm getting out and getting on with my life." Max is flushed with excitement at the prospect of her upcoming date that will follow this chore.

"At least let me dab the oil under your nose."

"Don't need it. I just have to not exit that tent in goose shit, and I'm a new girl."

In the glowing tent the lush smell of winter lilies greets Max's senses. It's so breathtaking that, were she there for any other reason, she would have teared up from the sheer saturation of sophisticated glitz. Huge chandeliers cast a scattered light that twinkles off the sterling silver decorations and clinking champagne flutes. On a stage at the far end of the tent Rihanna, in a hot, red Dior gown, croons a cool rendition of "White Christmas." Max steps behind a towering Christmas tree adorned with white orchids to pull open her clutch and check her phone. 8:40. Perfect. She'll find Hugo and his girlfriend, have a big, fat nothing exchange, wander, wander, wander, be the epitome of cool, calm, and collected—and we out.

She throws her shoulders back, takes a glass from a passing silver tray, and follows the chattering flow of jewel-toned velvet around the periphery of the dance floor. Blond guy—not him. Blond guy—not him. Blond guy—nope, *definitely* not him. Blond guy—insanely expensive custom-fitting tux. She scans for the gold family crest ring. Too far away to see it. She quickens her step as he strolls around one of the cocktail tables. Totally him! Him at three o'clock!

He sees her. He is all of ten feet away. Where is the girlfriend? She flattens her expression, turns her face to him, braced down to her plum-painted toes.

"Max?"

WHAT?

"Hugo," she says nonchalantly as she freezes for a second to regroup from the fact that he's not only acknowledging her but—sweet Jesus—lighting up.

"Hi." He crosses the final few feet until he's in front of her, smiling, his hands in his pockets like he just went out for an evening stroll and happened to be wearing a tux. "It's you." He grins. Why the talking?! And where is the girlfriend?! The *Post* promised her a girlfriend!

Turn away, she tells herself. *Turn and keep walking.* She does. But then he quickens his pace, his hands tugging from his pockets, to walk at her side. Not just talking to, but following her? WTF? This guy doesn't change his pace for anyone!

"I *thought* I saw you the other night," he says.

"Did you?" *Keep walking—but to where? The ladies' room. Go to the ladies' room!*

"At that Cabin place. But then I wasn't sure it was you. How are you?"

"Oh, busy, you know. I'm actually looking for the—" Someone pushes in front of her, and he puts a bracing hand on her bare arm to prevent a collision. And there's that damn heat that no amount of yacht-club rapping can extinguish. *Forget the ladies' room. Just get the hell out.*

"It feels kind of fated to see your name on the program tonight because I've been thinking about you," he says, lowering his face so his breath tingles her ear, his cologne fills her nose.

"You have." Max orients to the exit, and he steps closer. *Why did I turn down the oil?*

"I found my busted Harry Potter glasses the other day. I wanted to call you."

But you didn't, Max reminds herself. Max spots a waiter exiting through a side door. She's close to escape. "You know, it's great to see you and all, but I'm actually just stopping in before my date—"

Hugo grabs her arm as they both burst through the door and into an alley between the tent and the wrought-iron railing. "Do you think you could wait for a minute?"

"Okay, yes, you have exactly one." She tugs her arm back, daring to look up into his blue eyes, sparkling as they do when she's amusing him. "And that was it. Go back inside to your girlfriend, Hugo."

"My what?"

"Your date."

"Banishing me to an evening of dancing with my aunt? Heartless."

"I saw—I thought you had a girlfriend. Someone blond and boring."

"No such luck." He smiles. "That dress suits you. The peacock feathers." He eyes her, and she steps backward. "Always with that something extra, Max."

Max feels the cold metal of the railing make contact with the thin layer of silk. She's reached the edge. Out of the corner of her eye, she sees people walking on the sidewalk below.

Hugo places a hand on the railing to the left of her waist. He is looking at her like he used to, hungrily. The mantras of the last month plummet off the tip of her tongue and into a ravine of hormones. She's here because—because—"You dumped me, Hugo."

"I didn't." His other hand takes the railing on the right side of her. He's so close. "I didn't break up with you at all. When did I break up with you, tell me?"

"On the green. During a game, you—"

"*You* freaked out." He stares into her eyes. "And then you *seriously* freaked out and then you left. I think, technically, you left me."

"Because you were going out with Elizabeth Pendergast."

He moves his face closer. "Our parents have a vision. One of the things I always loved about you, Max, is that you got the obligations I have to my family are bullshit. And now you're shivering. Just . . . Let me." He presses his mouth to hers.

And he is Kryptonite incarnate.

Her body softens against his like a chiffon scarf fluttering to the ground. He grabs her ass, pressing her harder against him. The last year, the pain, the hurt, the humiliation, the exhaustion of working so hard to convince herself and everyone else she was over him, melts away in their entwined desire.

At the very same time, Ben approaches the corner where Max told him to meet her. He can't figure out why Bridget Stetson is standing there screaming at two people. "What the hell?!" she shouts. "She won't let me take Taylor back, but she can hook up with her ex?!"

Ben has no idea what's going on. As he gets closer he recognizes the guy Bridget's losing it at—the one he thought was Max's boyfriend.

"Well?!" Bridget screams. "Tell me!"

Zach doesn't look like he has any answers—he looks like he's going to hurl. Why does Zach know Bridget? And that girl next to Zach—she's the one who mushed that olive shit all over Taylor at the club. What's she doing here? Why is she crying?

"Bridget, what's going on?" Ben asks, and in response Bridget flings an accusatory finger at the railing above them . . . where Max is kissing some other guy.

"I love you," Hugo murmurs as his mouth moves down to Max's jaw, then her neck, finding that spot he always could, the one that lit up her spine. Consumed, she drops her head to the side—gasping when she takes in the street below them. "Shit, shit, shit," she cries, pushing Hugo away. "No!" she calls down. "It's not what you—" But she falters. It is exactly what they think.

Zach and Phoebe stare up at her with their hands over their mouths. Bridget's face is darkened with disgust, her eyes narrowed to slits. And there, standing in his father's tux, looking unquestionably like his heart has been broken, is Ben.

"Ben!" she calls.

He turns and starts to walk hurriedly away.

"Oh God." She runs back through the door into the tent, pushing through the crowd and servers and the tables, trying to get to the exit, Hugo right behind her. "Stop following me!" She blows past the girl holding out the parting goodie bags and lifts her dress to run down the carpeted stairs, her heel catching on a snag in the carpet. She stumbles to the asphalt in the departing taillights of the gypsy cab whisking Zach, Phoebe, and Bridget onto the West Side Highway. Max watches as Ben's figure breaks into a jog and disappears down the street in the opposite direction. Max drops her head, her shoulders shaking as the tears come.

The next thing she feels is the hot shock of Hugo's hand gently lacing into hers. She looks up as he crouches beside her, amazed her ragged emotional outburst hasn't scared him off. He lifts her to stand.

"You ended it." She struggles as tears snake down her cheeks. "And I made a new life for myself. Those are my friends. That was, what happened up there just now, that was a mistake."

"My mistake"—he cups her cheeks in his palms and searches her eyes for understanding—"was letting you go. Give me one night to make it up to you, Max. Please?

My car is waiting. It's warm in there. A few hours with me isn't going to change whatever I just walked into, is it? Do you really want to wonder forever if we could have gotten this back?"

CHAPTER 14

L ife is perfect, Max thinks as she rolls over in bed to watch the first rays of sunlight stream through the curtains the next morning. No crushing elephant, no leaf mold allergy, no giant boulder, which, with all her might and skill, she had shrunk to a pebble. But still. No one wants to walk around with a pebble in their shoe, much less their heart. It's kind of a binary system: pebble, no pebble. *And right now there is no pebble,* Max thinks as Hugo rolls over and wraps himself around her in his sleep—

Then, for a flash, Max feels something so much

worse. Like a bird raking its claws across her heart. She
sees Zach's stunned face. Bridget's disgust. Phoebe's tears.
Ben's shock.

No. She is not thinking about that now. She is thinking
about how great Hugo feels, the softness of his Egyptian
cotton sheets, the height of his apartment ceilings, the
scope of his penthouse view. *A view,* Max thinks, *I've been
missing a view.*

Hugo stretches awake and kisses her. "Hey, beautiful,"
he says. "I'm glad you stayed."

"Well, it was such a great dress, I'd hate to do my
walk of shame in the wee hours when no one could
appreciate it."

"I've missed you." He laughs, pulling her closer. She
can't believe she's here. In his bed, in his arms, in his *life.*
She feels so awake. She can't believe how much energy
trying to pretend she didn't miss him had been sucking
out of her. He kisses her forehead. "Mmm, and how your
hair smells," he says.

"Thank you—"

"I'm starving." He sits and picks up his phone. "You
starving?"

"Yes," she says, realizing, now that he's suggested it,
she is.

"Hey, it's Tillman across the street. Yeah. I'll take
two western omelets, whites only, whole wheat toast, no

potatoes, and two coffees. Thanks."

Not what she would have ordered *at all*, but fine. She spots his shirt from the night before and scoops it from the floor.

"You don't have lotion on, do you?" he asks, pulling up his jeans.

"Not anymore," she says coyly.

"Okay, just 'cause certain drugstore lotions can discolor French cotton."

"Um," she says, still not sure if he's kidding. "I don't think I'm wearing anything—staining."

"Cool. Listen, help yourself to a shower. I just need to email in a paper." He drops down at his desk chair and opens his laptop. "Today's gonna be a little crazy, and I don't want to forget."

"Oh?" Max asks.

"Yeah, the last permit came through on the Tribeca project and the launch party's tonight. The last bit of fun, then it's all hard hats and sewage lines." Hugo makes a face like he used to on the rare occasion he had to take the Greyhound home from school. "You gonna take that shower?"

"Yes." She crosses to the marble bathroom, her eyes bugging when she sees a box of tampons sitting on the toilet tank.

"There's a bunch of my sister's shit in there so you

should be able to find everything you need!" he calls.

"Right," she says to herself as she turns on the rain shower. The water feels amazing. But as Max steps under the pounding spray all she can hear in the pulsing silence is Ben asking her out for a real date—

Max turns off the water, wrapping herself in an ankle-length bath sheet as she hears Hugo in the living room paying the delivery guy. She pads out to find him dropping the foil take-out containers on the mango wood dining table. "Not bad digs for a freshman."

"Yeah, I wasn't slumming in campus housing when we have this place," he says. "Kirsten has the other room, but she's never here. I don't know—I probably have a dorm somewhere—there's some guy out there who's stoked to have a single. That's kind of charity, right?"

"Just keep telling yourself that," Max says drily as she walks over. "I'm just surprised—I really thought you hated New York."

"I hated my parents' New York. The stuffy galas. The dismal Harvard Club dinners. Now that I'm here on my own, I love it. The people, the mess, the energy."

"Me too! I'm really impressed you did it. That must have been no small fight."

"Yeah." He nods, his eyes wandering to the sideboard. "Put on some music?"

Max scrolls through his iPod, but can't find the album

she's looking for. "Hey, where're Florence and the Machine?"

"Ugh, not that shit."

"But we listened to them all the time," Max says, confused as she recalls long afternoons studying in his room as she DJed his iPod.

"That was Deacon's iPod."

"What?"

"Yeah. Why would you think that was mine?"

"I didn't realize, between going vegan and wearing a hemp field-hockey uniform, that your roommate was into material possessions." Her thumb goes a few more ticks round the dial, but she doesn't see OK Go, or even Mumford & Sons. She sees a lot of rap about Glocks and bitches and some heavy metal about heat and whores. Okay, then.

"Your food's getting cold," he says, patting the chair next to him.

A call comes in on his phone, and he lets it go to voice mail, then listens to it, his mouth pinching as he rolls his eyes to the ceiling. "My mom thinks every time she has to be in town I can drop everything for a mother-son day. A little chance for her to give me some 'feedback.'" He looks over at her, an idea seeming to occur to him. "Hey, why don't you two have lunch together?"

"Us?"

"Sure! She likes you. Go get your hair done—I'll have her buy you something to wear tonight—and I'll meet you guys at the party. You game?" he asks. "I just have a ton to get done."

"Oh, wow. Okay, great. But I, uh, only have my gown here." And she's guessing peacock feathers and Mrs. Tillman don't seem well matched.

"Check Kirsten's closet. She's a little shorter than you, but you should be able to find something. And seriously, take whatever. Like I said, never here."

Max watches him carve up his egg whites, not able to believe it—not only has she stepped right back into being his girlfriend as if no time had passed, he now wants her to hang out with his mom.

After breakfast, while Hugo showers and dresses, Max rifles through his older sister's closet. She finds a pair of black slim-cut pants where the gap at her ankle will look deliberate, which she pairs with a white blouse and nubby Chanel blazer. Kirsten's feet are a little bigger than Max's but she finds a pair of red ballet flats and stuffs the toe with tissue paper. Of course Kirsten doesn't have any makeup, but Max's lips are still red from the impact of Hugo's and she hopes being out in the cold will flush her cheeks. When she's done Max looks in the mirror and thinks that, minus the racy flash of ankle, she looks like one of the mothers at St. Something's.

"Max!" Hugo calls. "You ready yet?"

"Coming!"

She finds him in jeans and a blazer at the front door, already ajar. He does a double take when he sees her.

"What?" she asks.

"You look like Kirsten."

"Is that a—I just thought—lunch with your mom."

"No, right, can't exactly send you in there in your red boots." He laughs to himself as the buzzer rings. "Okay, that's the car to take you to her hotel. Come on."

She grabs her clutch and follows him to the elevator, where they ride down thirty stories. She's waiting for him to take her hand, take her face, even push the emergency break and just—take her. But he doesn't.

"Okay," he says, walking briskly out the lobby like they do this every day, like this is just who they are, which is better, Max thinks, than swooping kisses and quick passion. This is forever. "See you tonight."

Seated beneath the gilt ceiling of the Waldorf Astoria, Mrs. Tillman picks up one of the strange tiny silver implements on the side of her plate and starts to poke her lobster salad. Max peers down at the array of things beside her own plate that look like buttonhooks and nose-hair trimmers and tries to figure out which one she is supposed to use on the escargots Mrs. Tillman insisted she try.

Max glances again at the empty chair across from them, the little rosette of raw tuna congealing as it awaits Mrs. Tillman's friend's arrival. "So, Maxine," Mrs. Tillman says warmly. "I wasn't expecting to see you again. What a—treat. Are you at university this year?"

"I'm applying now." Max gamely takes hold of one of the shells with the tongs the server handed her and picks up the buttonhook.

"And did you run into Hugo at an alumnae event?"

"No. Something at the High Line," she says vaguely, not sure the details of the benefit will sound glamorous to her or distastefully gauche in their flashiness. "Do you know it? The new park."

Mrs. Tillman gives a barely perceptible shudder, the idea of meeting in a park seeming to conjure Max playing a guitar in front of an open case for spare change. "Oh, yes, well, I suppose that is the thing about being down here—you could cross paths with *anyone*. Not like back at home, where the community is culled somewhat. I still have *no idea* why Hugo's father insisted he give up Harvard for this."

"It was his father's idea?" Max asks, trying to keep her voice from cracking.

"Yes." She pokes her salad. "The board is obsessive about this whole notion of becoming a twenty-first-century company, and Hugo Senior wants to keep them happy, prove that the family can stay at the helm. Little Hugo doesn't really have a say in the matter." She touches her pearls.

"Oh," Max says, knowing if he were here right now he would be clenching his jaw at his detested moniker. Did he lie to her this morning—or just not set her straight?

"There she is."

As Max replays her conversation with Hugo she realizes the woman crossing the restaurant looks famil-iar. Despite being twenty minutes late, she doesn't rush past the starched tablecloths and elaborate centerpieces. "Vivian," she addresses Mrs. Tillman. "Apologies. The traffic in this city is appalling." She unnecessarily touches her headband to straighten it, as if she came in a con-vertible.

"Sloane," Mrs. Tillman greets her in return. "You remember Maxine from school?"

"No, I can't say that I do. Were you in Elizabeth's class?"

"Which Elizabeth?" Of the three in her class, the two the year ahead, and the four the year behind.

"Maxine," Mrs. Tillman says simply, "this is Mrs. Dow Pendergast."

Suddenly the bread sticks in Max's throat like sand. "So nice to meet you," Max rasps as Sloane seats herself with no mention of Max as Hugo's girlfriend forthcoming. Max takes a sip of water. "I was one class under. How is Elizabeth?" She forces herself to ask, because she knows that's as required as getting these slugs down. She hopes the answer is "married to a pygmy and living in Papua New Guinea."

"Oh, good. Enjoying Princeton. She wasn't sure she'd like it as much as Yale, but in the end it was all about cutting down her commute time into the city." Sloane gives Vivian a knowing smile. *Elizabeth isn't coming in to go shopping,* Max thinks, *and she definitely isn't all about the food. She's coming to see Hugo.*

She's his princess.

After a blessedly brief lunch, the remainder of which centered around horse breeding and the Boston Symphony, Max enters the hair salon with Vivian, still feeling the blood swoosh in her ears. Okay, maybe he was seeing Elizabeth—but that was before he saw Max. Before the perfection of last night. *Hugo doesn't tell his mother anything,* Max reminds herself, trying to think rationally.

Max decides better to wait until after the mani/pedi, the facial, the blowout, until Hugo sees her tonight in all her glory again, done to the nines, his eyes locked on her with that look of hunger and adoration. As soon as she's sure of her footing, she'll ask. *Why pull me back into your life, your* bed, *if Elizabeth is already in it?*

As the limousine ferries them downtown to the party, Max thinks, *This is so not the nines.* This isn't even done to the sevens or fives. Max wishes she could give one last glance at her appearance in her compact, but since the chances that she's grown makeup or Blake Lively waves since she and Mrs. Tillman were ushered directly from the salon to the backseat of the town car are slim, what's the point? After four hours at Kenneth, she and Mrs. Tillman have emerged looking exactly the same as when they went in, except, perhaps, with clearer pores. Max smoothes down the front of the shapeless silk sack dress, trying to give it a waist with static cling. She crosses her ankles, not able to believe she's still wearing the ballet flats. Max tried to suggest swinging by the Saks shoe department, but when Mrs. Tillman said, "Oh for God's sake, who's going to be looking at your feet?" Max let it drop. That is such a not–New York thing to say.

"You look lovely, dear," Vivian addresses her for the first time in an hour.

"Thank you. And thank you for the dress," Max manages. "I love it."

"My pleasure. Kirsten doesn't let me shop for her anymore, and it's so fun picking out things that are youthy." Yes, so youthy, this borderline maternity dress. "And," Vivian adds, "it's a much better look than those things you used to wear, if you don't mind my saying." She reaches across the leather divide and squeezes Max's hand, perhaps unaware of her words' sting. Her "feedback," Max thinks, grateful she actually hadn't had more opportunities to get to know Vivian last year—as she had once hoped. "So, dear, where are you applying to college?" She pulls her hand back to smooth her velvet jacket.

"Actually, NYU," Max says, so glad to finally have the road forward be obstacle-free.

"I beg your pardon?" Vivian coughs into her hand.

"Would you like some water?" Max picks up one of the tiny bottles in the armrest.

"No, thank you." Vivian seems to shift her body away from her. "I didn't realize you had your sights set on going to college with Hugo."

"It wasn't like that—didn't happen in that order—"

"You know, I met Mr. Tillman in college. I was at Radcliffe when the merger with Harvard started. These are very important years for Hugo—making contacts—and impressions."

"No, of course."

"Pity he seems so determined to get a rise out of us."

With a shiver, Max realizes Vivian is referring to her as the car rolls to a stop in front of the aisle of photographers flanking the red carpet. Immediately someone opens the door and extends a hand to Mrs. Tillman, who doesn't wait for Max, leaving her to walk the carpet alone. She can hear the paparazzi asking each other who she is and is she worth wasting the memory on. She tries to get to the woman with the clipboard as fast as possible. "Max Scott," she tells her.

"I'm sorry," the woman says, looking up. "Could it be under another name?"

"Yes, right, I'm Hugo Tillman's plus one." Saying it, Max feels the warm rush she has missed all day.

The woman flips to the *T* page and her brow furrows. "Um, I'm sorry, he doesn't have a plus one."

"That must be a mistake—I came with Mrs. Tillman—I was in her car—she can vouch for me." They both look into the party pavilion, but Vivian is gone. Max turns back to the clipboard woman as it starts to snow. "Could you maybe send someone to go find Hugo?"

"I'll see what I can do—wait here."

Max does. By the entrance. Like she's a lost intern from the PR firm of Frump & Dowdy. Max sends a text, "Here! ☺" Ten minutes turn into twenty. Twenty turns into thirty. Max is getting frozen. Max is getting annoyed.

Just then another town car pulls up and out climbs the Pendergast clan. Perfectly, impeccably blah. Mr. Pendergast and Mrs. Pendergast lead the way in matching camel-colored cashmere topcoats and brush right past Max as if Sloane hadn't dined across from her mere hours ago. "Max?" Elizabeth's voice drips with fake shock as she gives Max an obvious once-over. Under her own camel coat, Elizabeth's wearing a similarly shapeless dress. "*What* are you doing here?"

"I could ask you the same thing."

Elizabeth leans in, smile in place. "My mother told me she ran into you, and I got on the first train. I heard you were in a funny farm somewhere."

"Time off for good behavior." Max holds her ground.

Elizabeth narrows her eyes. "Are you going in?"

"Momentarily," she answers, willing it.

"Max!" They both turn their heads as Hugo barrels through the entrance. "Elizabeth!" he calls with obvious shock, breaking on the heels of his patent Belgian loafers. He tries to re-form his features into a smile. "I wasn't expecting you! What a treat!"

Elizabeth smiles smugly, then looks around, her purse held in both hands. "You made this party sound boring.

If I'd known it was going to be a *reunion* I'd have told you I'd come."

Hugo looks uncharacteristically thrown. "It is boring. So not worth your traveling in from school."

"You know I love to be supportive." She raises her eyebrows. "Oh, look, there are *so* many people in there I know and really should go say hello to. And there's my father with his arm around your father." She turns to Max. "It was great to see you. Since I don't expect to again, I'll wish you well now." She turns away and, with a passing predatory smile to Hugo, walks inside.

Max and Hugo stare at each other, the snow falling between them.

"Am I?" Max asks, her teeth starting to chatter, as his mother's words really sink in.

"Are you what?"

"Just a way to get back at your parents for forcing you to be like the six hundred Hugos before you."

"No! Where the hell did you—no." He steps close to her. "You're my Max, you know that. You're special." She nods. She is. "But I have responsibilities. I mean, it's not like I kept that from you, right? We're not in high school anymore. You can be grown-up about this, can't you?" He places his hand on the base of her neck, extending his fingers under her hair. "I have to do things for my family. But you're the one I want to be with. This thing with Elizabeth—" He lowers his voice. "I will get out of it. Of course. It's just that—I haven't had the heart to break it to her yet," he whispers.

And there it is—the look of hunger, of adoration, the look she has been craving all day—all year.

And she feels nothing.

Better than nothing.

His gold signet ring is caught in her hair. His breath smells like crab puffs. And feeling she's the one, while thinking she's not good enough to be the one, is just plain not good enough.

Max steps back. "Oh my God."

"What?"

"I'm special?" She raises her arms to shoulder height, her voice getting louder. "You have. No. Idea."

"Max, calm down."

"I am calm. That's the crazy thing. Anger would mean I cared. And, wow, I really don't." She looks at him, suddenly seeing nose pores and a stubble strip and how one of his eyes is actually slightly smaller than the other. She takes a breath, carefully choosing her last words. "You'll toe the Tillman line, while rolling your eyes, just like you toed the St. Something's line. As if constantly saying 'it's all bullshit' somehow excuses your behavior. It doesn't. You always love that I voice my opinion, except when it's about us or, more precisely, you. But here it is: never taking a stand on anything doesn't make you 'responsible' or 'mature'—it makes you a coward. When I met you, I was a girl with a whole lot of talk, but since you dumped me—"

He goes to protest, but Max barrels over him. "Or just cheated on me and I 'flipped out'—whichever— I'm now a girl committed to walk that talk. I want to be with someone who does the brave thing. Especially if that brave thing is wanting to be with me—for real. Here's the most important takeaway for you: you may *not* live vicariously through my courage. You get the life you deserve, Hugo, and I'm certain you will have a very blah one.

"And," she adds, "I'm still applying to NYU. Because it's *my* vision for building *my* life. Leave my Carolina Herrera in your lobby and tell your mom I'll send a messenger to swap it for this dress tomorrow—it's shapeless and awful and I'm sure Kirsten will love it."

He looks so bewildered. "That's it? You're going?" he asks, even after everything she's said.

She shakes her head. It may be years before he understands. He may be paunchy and bald and sitting on the floor of an apartment his ex-wife's movers are emptying before he suddenly gets, "Oh. People can *leave* me."

"Bye, Hugo. Have a nice life." Max elbows her way through the arriving guests, desperate to get free of these people. She finally makes it to the end of the red carpet and strides onto the clear sidewalk toward home. Then she knows it through her whole body: *I am free.*

I am over him.

CHAPTER 15

The triumphant feeling lasts exactly one subway ride. And then it hits her like she walked into a wall of fuck. "Fuuuuuuuuck," she says out loud. Behind her eyes is a slide show of awful. Everyone standing on the street below as Hugo kissed her last night. Phoebe. Zach. The recognition between Ben and Bridget. And then there's Taylor Bradley, who she really may have given a nervous breakdown. After what she selfishly did last night to Ben, who was she to be so judgmental? She walks from the train, fighting the feeling that her stomach is trying to escape down to the pavement and slink away, too ashamed to belong to her anymore.

As she turns the corner and sees her house she prays that the light might be on in her windows, that Zach and Phoebe might be inside, waiting to chalk it all up to Kryptonite and move forward. Or even waiting to rip her a new one. But at least there. Instead she finds it empty as she unlocks her door. She sits at her desk and pulls her phone from her clutch. At least she didn't miss any new Hour Ones since last night, thank God. But there are a fair amount of last-minute "I might see him at this Christmas party" voice mails that came in while she was under Mrs. Tillman's oppressive wing today. She wants to cry, but knows she can't possibly collapse under the weight of these feelings right now. There's no time for that. She slips out of that assaholic dress, kicks off those assaholic flats, and tugs on jeans and a T-shirt. She pulls up her hair, makes a pot of coffee, grabs a fresh pack of markers, and pulls out the rolling white board. None of which is any substitution for having a team.

But Max needs a plan.

Ben stares into the greasy bottom of the fried chicken bucket, and burps, realizing he feels no less miserable than when he made a KFC run an hour ago. Only now he's sad *and* nauseous. He can't get his brain to move off those sickening minutes under the High Line last night—as that guy kissed Max, and Ben pieced together what had happened to Taylor from Bridget's angry tirade at Zach and that girl. Both of whom, he now realizes, he has to think of as Max's evil minions. He drops the bucket on his bedside table, pauses the DVR, and lays back to stare at the ceiling, allowing airtime to the questions he tried to muffle with chicken and football. How could he have been such a fucking idiot? The city's full of perfectly nice girls, why did he have to pick the one who capsized his best friend and got with someone else right in front of him? Every time the image comes back of that douchey guy inhaling her face, he just wants to—

Ben leaps off his bed, lunges across the room, and gets to the toilet just in time to deposit the extra-crispy six-piece dinner.

Empty, he sits back on the tile and wipes his mouth with the bottom of a towel. He rests his head against the cold wall. And then he allows himself to ask the worst question of all: If she sucks so much, why can't he just stop thinking about her?

The next morning, after staying up until dawn strategizing, Max gets to Bergdorf's Men's a half hour before the store opens, clutching the pre-Christmas sale ad from the Sunday *Times*. She knows in her bones that Zach will come through at some point today. She positions herself on the corner of 58th for the stakeout. From her spot, she can see down the avenue to the main entrance and simultaneously east to the side entrance. She's ready.

Within a few minutes of manning the corner she's seeing her breath and appreciating Zach and Phoebe even more, if that's possible. If this was an ex, she thinks, Phoebe could watch the front entrance from the warmth of the women's store across the street and Zach could have the side covered from under the heat blowers of the Apple Store entrance, so Max could be waiting for their "go" over hot chocolate at the Plaza.

She gives herself permission to cross to the side of the street with the hot dog vendors, so she can at least stand in the wake of their steam. But an hour goes by and her feet are numb and she smells like meat soaking in water and still no sign of Zach.

"Frug," she murmurs, before dashing over to the store in hopes of finding a spot *inside* that will give her a view of both entrances. Once past the revolving door Max stomps her boots on the taupe carpet. The employees watch apprehensively as the trickle of shoppers becomes a steady flow of eager bargain chasers, their faces as braced as defensive linemen. Max maneuvers to the necktie rotunda, where she can see everyone entering.

But another hour and she is getting dangerously close to peeing on herself. Now she gets why that astronaut wore a diaper. Urgent missions and pee breaks do not mix. *When does James Bond pee?* she wonders. At the triggering thought of Ben, her throat closes for a moment, but she breathes through it.

She rushes through dress shirts, past the sock section, to the bespoke alcove, running the back stairs to the top floor ladies' lounge. Where she is on line behind every wife and girlfriend who seems to be choosing this moment in the mirrored stalls to ask themselves if they should start coloring their hair.

Max bobs her knees, looking at her watch. Even if he slept in, met Tom for brunch, Zach should still be here while the getting's good. Finally a stall door opens and she runs in.

Max flies back down and across the floor so fast she can't brake on the marble mosaic and her hips slam into the cuff link case. The salesman clears his throat and she gives him an apologetic smile—before something catches her eye. She spins around, looking past the sea of felt fedoras and oversized fur hats. Suddenly she glimpses the heel of a sneaker as it passes out of view up the grand staircase. She shimmies through the shoppers, but by the time she gets to the second-floor landing he's gone again. She jostles her way through the crowds down the corridor of boutiques. At the end, she doubles back and fights up one more flight. And there, trying on a skintight, short-sleeved seersucker blazer and matching hot pants from Thom Browne's resort collection, is Zach.

"No," Max huffs, dropping her hands to her thighs as she crouches, catching her breath. "I came here to apologize and I want to get on your good side, but I still can't let you buy that."

Zach turns slowly from the mirror, raising the Jackie O sunglasses he grabbed to complete the look. "Bite me."

"*Come on.* I've had this place staked out since nine thirty. At least talk to me."

He purses his lips. "Your powers of deduction are impressive. I mean, I didn't shackle my fortunes to yours because you were mediocre." He mists up and drops the glasses back down on his nose.

"Good to hear?" she tries, relieved he's at least thinking of her as a boss, if not a best friend. That's something.

"Were. It's all in the past now, Baby Jane."

"It doesn't have to be."

"Hot cider?" A gentleman cuts in proffering a tray.

"Thank you." Max takes two cups and hands one off. "Look, I know I handled Hugo *really* badly. Like, needs a new word for *badly*, badly."

"You turned your back on everything you stand for.

And you left Phoebe and me holding the bag with Basket Case Bridget and Double-0 Hottie."

"That was a mistake."

"You're not engaged to the Tillmans?" He studies her.

"No. We're not anything. I told him I was going to NYU, and he could kiss my ass."

"So I don't need to come up with a new best friend while you go MIA?"

"No! Zach, why would you even say that?"

"Do you have any idea what it's like to be out in high school? I wear it with a winning sense of humor and rakish sense of style, but it's not easy."

"I know, I mean, you've told me." She nods.

"What you don't know is that I brought a guy to the fall formal last year. We had a great time. No one was rude to our faces. But when we went to get our coats, someone had cracked eggs in the pockets. Of my Armani!" He drops his head and pretends to look at something on the carpet but Max knows better.

"Zach, I had no idea."

"Exactly." He pulls back, wiping under his eyes. "Because you were busy at boarding school. I felt like I couldn't talk to you."

"You should have called me!"

"And say what? Obviously you've dropped me, but

I'm dealing with some ignorant fuckwads and could use a pep talk?"

"But I *didn't* drop you! I think I didn't tell you about Hugo because . . . because deep down I always knew something was a little off about the whole thing. It was too good—or as it turned out, too bad—to be true. He wasn't really into me, he was into the fact that I could say what I thought when he couldn't. You'd have picked up on that right away. But I was so lonely, Zach. I felt like I couldn't risk you pricking my Hugo bubble. Seriously, I would have taken attention from a mass murderer at that point. God, I'm so sorry. What happened after the formal? Did it get worse? Did they find who did it?"

"I didn't report it—"

"Zach—"

"But then you showed up." He stares at her, shrugging. "I got my swagger back, and it stopped. I don't know. Maybe they moved on to tormenting someone else."

"I should have been there for you," Max says.

He pulls off the shades. "You look like shit. Not worried you're going to run into Hugo?"

"I've told you I don't care anymore. You guys got me over him, you know, with an untraditional detour through my Moment. But there's no way I would've arrived on the other side without you. Making it right with you and Phoebe is all I care about."

"As I recall you left a larger body count."

"I know," Max acknowledges, holding up her phone to show him she actually made a list.

Zach looks down at the screen. "He's next. Good." Zach nods, satisfied. "Oh my God, Dr. Schmidt is tomorrow?!" His eyes bug as he sees the last item.

"I'm so screwed. Zach," Max says, so relieved to be talking to him again, but so unsure of the future. "Are we okay?"

Zach stares at a mannequin in a poncho for a full minute. Finally, as Max reaches out to take his hand, he turns back. "I appreciate you coming by here and all, but I need some time to think," Zach says seriously. "I still don't really know if you get it or this is just a big, fat half ass in disguise."

At that moment, Phoebe rounds the corner with an armful of things for Zach to try on. The very sight of Max makes her look like someone just slapped her.

"Phoebe?" Max entreats. "Zach?"

"I need time," he answers. Phoebe nods in agreement. "We need time."

* * *

Needing to keep moving until it feels like *something* in this shit mess has been put right, Max knocks. "I'm coming," an exasperated voice says on the other side. Girded, Max digs her fingernails into her palms to keep from running down the block.

A little girl opens the door.

"Hi, I'm looking for Taylor?" Max says.

"Did he win something?" She holds on to the doorknob with both hands.

"No."

"Is he in trouble?"

"How old do you think I am?" Max asks.

"I don't know." The girl tilts her head and appraises her subject. "Thirty?"

"That does it, I need to start moisturizing. No, he isn't a millionaire and, no, he isn't headed to jail, I just need to talk to him."

"Taylor, get out of bed!" She turns to the stairs and shouts up. "There's a pretty lady here to see you!"

Having come straight from Bergdorf's, Max thinks that's a generous assessment. She bites her lip as she waits. Even now, weeks after The Moment, Taylor is still showing up to pursue Bridget. And, now that Max finally sees Hugo for who he really is or—more to the point—isn't, she has to admit he never even came close to showing up for her, not even once. Which means because of her own baggage, Max gave Bridget the wrong advice.

Taylor walks heavily down the stairs in his sweats. She barely recognizes him from that night at the Cabin. His eyes are hollowed and he could use a shave.

"Yeah?" He hunches his shoulders, pushing his hands into his pockets as he comes to the door.

"Taylor, hi. I'm Max Scott."

"Why do I know your name?"

"Um, well, you probably heard about me from Ben. I'm here because—"

"The mystery chick who messed with Bridget and cheated on my best friend?" He glares at her. "What, are you here to kill my cat, too?"

"Okay, first, I'm not here to talk about Ben. I'm here to talk about Bridget. Who I did not mess with. Yes, I stopped her from listening to your apologies. And I feel really bad about that, but you have to see it from my perspective. You dumped her. Cruelly and out of nowhere."

"He did," Daisy agrees.

Taylor cringes. "I was losing my nerve when she started to cry. I harshed on her to keep from changing my mind. It wasn't cool."

Daisy shakes her head.

"My gig was to take care of her after you broke her heart," Max continues. "Would you really have advised her, in my shoes, to give you a second chance?"

Embarrassed, he can't look at her.

"But you persevered. And at a certain point I should've allowed that maybe you genuinely regretted your decision."

"I did! I do," he says earnestly, and then clams up. "I'm not going into this."

Daisy elbows him.

"Look, here's the thing," Max says, feeling so bad about all of it, just needing to get to the point already. "Bridget really likes you. I think you should give it one more try."

"Thanks for the endorsement, but she won't even talk to me. I've emailed and texted, I sent her a song, I got Daisy to follow her on Twitter—"

"Taylor, I've gotten out of the way." Max opens her red bag and pulls out a small bunch of wildflowers tied at the base with a silk ribbon. "Here. Walk across the street. Ring the doorbell. Talk to her. Be honest. It's really that simple. Trust me. I'm a girl."

And as she says it she prays the same holds true for boys.

Max swings by the deli on her way home, but Ben isn't there. It was a long shot, she says to herself as she squints down Court Street. But even from this far away she can see the lights of Cooper Baby are off on this late

Sunday afternoon. She knows she should just walk down there, pound the window, make him talk to her. But she doesn't think she can take one more person looking at her today like she's stuck to the bottom of their shoe.

Max descends the stairs, ready with cereal to tackle the next name on her list. Dr. Schmidt. Whose socks Max needs to knock off first thing tomorrow morning. "Okay!" Max says out loud to galvanize herself as she fires up the laptop, pretending her team is there with her. "I'm going to just put the finishing touches on this presentation, maybe kill a goat in the backyard for good luck, and I am good to go."

In a short while, the goat thing is seeming like it might be her best bet. Zach has all the files organized according to Zach logic. Which don't seem to match Phoebe's statistics. The data is, to Max's eyes, a mess. And Max's accompanying presentation paper needs *serious* work. This is a week away from being done, at best. How could she have wasted this last weekend?!

"Max!" her mother shouts down the stairs. "Is that you? Why weren't you answering your phone? I didn't know where you were!"

"What?" Max asks, struggling to absorb her mother's anger.

"You missed my office Christmas party!" Anne comes puffing down the sagging steps. "You should have told me you weren't going to come by."

Max points at her computer. "Fine."

"You should have called."

"Fine."

"We're having dinner tonight at the table."

"Fine."

"Please don't keep 'fine-ing' me," Anne levels at her.

Max slams her pen down. "You're ready to play house. I get it. But don't expect me to pretend to be a kid again."

"Except you *are* still a kid, Max. And I won't have you abusing my confidence."

"What are you talking about?"

"I know you didn't come home Friday night."

"How?"

"Because I checked on you."

"*Now* you're checking on me?" Max's head pounds.

"Max?"

"*I've* abused your confidence?" Max is incredulous, her anger breaking. "How about you've abused *mine*. Throwing me all over the country. I know, you were young, you did the best you could. But it sucked, Mom, it sucked. I always told myself this was the best you and Dad are capable of, but it isn't!" She points at her mom's stomach.

"You *could* settle down, make a life, I just wasn't important enough to do it for." The force of her tears surprises them both.

"Oh, Max, of course you were important." Anne shakes her head as she takes this in, her tone softening. "You're the most important thing in my life."

"Not anymore."

"You will always be my number one. You amaze me! You're so independent. You seemed to settle in everywhere so well. I never worried about you."

"I know!"

"That's not what I mean. Well, maybe it is," she concedes.

"I want someone to worry about me!"

Max's mom just stands there with her hands over her mouth.

"I want someone to do for me what I do for my clients."

"Your *who*?" her mother asks.

"My clients," Max says simply.

"What are you talking about?"

"Okay, I'm not an escort. But you might want to sit down for this."

By the time Max has filled her mother in on every last detail, Anne is stunned, embarrassed, concerned—and impressed. "So this Dr. Schmidt has agreed to meet with you tomorrow?" she asks from where she's curled on the chaise.

"Yes. But I'm so not ready." Max blows her nose, realizing this may all have been for nothing. She may still end up busing tables at the Newark airport Chili's. "I'm *nowhere* near ready."

Just then, they both hear a key in the lock and see Zach and Phoebe standing in the doorway. Zach looks over at Anne.

"Go ahead," Max says. "She knows."

"Okay, then, here are our terms," Zach begins.

"Anything," Max says, restraining herself from running to throw herself at their sneakers.

"No more skeletons in the closet. You know I detest a closet."

"Done."

"Seriously. You spring another car accident on this business you're on your own, professionally. You disappear again, you're on your own, period." Zach points a finger at her to show he's not joking.

"Of course."

"And I want a promotion." Phoebe crosses her arms.

"Oh—"

"I ran your recovery, Max. I'm ready."

"Hmm . . . is there room in this room for two firsts?"

By way of an answer, Phoebe blows past Max and

Anne to the laptop, opening her bag and pulling out a box of Mallomars, her preferred late-night stimulant.

"We're on Christmas break," Zach announces as he tosses off his coat. "And we're prepared to work on this till dawn if we need to."

"What did you do to the data?" Phoebe asks, horrified.

"I was trying to put the charts in an order—"

"No, you messed it all up. Give me five minutes, I can have this back together."

"Well, I can see you're in good hands." Anne stands, and Max gets up to walk her to the stairs. "And after that pitch I'd sure as hell want you at my school."

"You're biased." Max smiles.

"I am. Max, you have twelve more hours to shine this thing. We thrive under deadline. I'll bring you guys dinner. You're due a little coddling." She pulls Max into her arms and gives her a reassuring hug.

As Anne walks back up the stairs, Max looks from Phoebe to Zach, tears of gratitude springing to her eyes. "Thank you, guys."

Zach pulls out the memory stick with the latest version of her presentation. "And I will concede that, yes, *maybe* I would have pricked your bubble."

"Zachary," Max gushes, throwing her arms around him. "I love the prick in you."

* * *

If Zach was just being gallant by offering to stay, he never shows it as midnight meets the wee hours meets the sun. On her second back-to-school all-nighter, Max is past the point where caffeine can sharpen her, past the point where Corn Pops can adrenalize her. As she gets out of the subway station to walk over to the psychology department with Zach and Phoebe, Max is giggling—stoned on fear.

"Don't focus on the lack of recidivism," Zach coaches her as Phoebe smoothes Max's hair. "Focus on the overall success rate. Keep coming back to the numbers on page twelve and make sure she sees the graphs."

Max nods, no longer hearing any of it.

"Okay," Phoebe says, "this is the place."

Max turns to them. "I can't do this."

"You can."

"What if I snow this doctor into thinking I know what I'm talking about, and I take this program national, and it's like that cholesterol medication they just recalled? What if I do more harm than good? What if I *don't* know what I'm doing? What about Bridget?" She finally says the name out loud. "I got that *so* wrong. That was, like, breakup malpractice."

Zach turns Max's head to see Bridget waiting by the entrance.

"A little birdie in a tartan jacket told me you had a

big thing here today," Bridget says.

"I owe you such an apology—"

"Yeah, I was really mad at you. For lying to me." Bridget ticks off on her fingers. "And having a double standard, and just generally screwing up my life."

"Totally fair."

"But then I realized, you didn't. If you'd never come along, I'd still be crying on my bedroom floor, writing love poems to Taylor in shaving cream on my window, and just generally being a mess. Your program *works*. And I want it to keep working. Taylor and I are back together. And it may be the real deal. And it may just be a big, fat half ass in disguise. But if it is, I'll be sad, but, ultimately, I'll be okay. I know that now. I'm not Angie Riverdale."

"I am," Max says gravely.

"Duh." She throws her arms around Max. "Now go get some university cred to take this thing global!"

Buoyed by that hug, Max somehow finds herself in front of Dr. Jane Schmidt, trying to present her findings and sell herself. "So, if you look at page twelve, you'll see I've compiled a graph."

But Dr. Schmidt only nods halfheartedly, flips a few pages, ends up on one that is *not* twelve, and looks up as if to say, "Continue." *Oh God, I'm losing her,* Max thinks. This is a disaster. Max starts to sweat. She moves on to talking about the behavioral psychology elements she's incorporated into the program, but she can tell she still doesn't have Dr. Schmidt's attention. "And that's, I guess, really it, then, so, yeah," Max winds down with a lackluster finish.

Dr. Schmidt doesn't say anything.

"Dr. Schmidt?" Max asks.

"Sorry." She pushes her glasses up into her auburn hair, and Max can see she's been crying.

"Are you okay?"

"Why don't you leave your paper with me and I'll try to find time to look through it over the holidays." Max grips her chair as she feels her future, local and global, slip away.

"Okay, thank you for your time." Max gathers up her support materials and hands them off. "I love that watch," Max says, admiring the same gold Michael Kors one she had borrowed a few weeks ago.

"Thanks. My fiancé gave it to me." Dr. Schmidt sucks in her lips. Max's eyes dart to Dr. Schmidt's ring finger to see that it is barren, with just a faint tan line where the band must have been.

"I'm so sorry," Max says as she stands with her bag.

"No, *I'm* sorry." She furiously tries to wipe her cheeks dry. "I should have taken the week off. My fiancé—" The words seem to get stuck in her throat as she tries to stand to see Max out. *"Is leaving me for someone in the French department."*

"Oh, Jane." Without even realizing what she's doing, Max lowers Dr. Schmidt back into her chair. She automatically opens her red bag and pulls out her thermos, her pillbox, her chocolate, placing each on the table until she catches herself. "Sorry, I don't mean to presume." Max starts to put them back. "I've only worked with girls. And obviously being engaged is hardly going out for a few months—"

Dr. Schmidt puts her hand on Max's to stop her from repacking. "It can't make it any worse."

"That's actually one of our mottos." Max sheepishly unwraps the candy bar and hands it to her.

"What would you say next?" She takes it from Max. "If I was a teenager."

"That it hurts," Max acknowledges and Jane nods gratefully, mouth full of chocolate as Max ventures to continue with building confidence. "Mornings and evenings are the worst. But every day there's going to be a little window of time where you feel not just 'barely alive,' not just 'okay,' but positively euphoric. Winning *American Idol* euphoric. And that window, offering you a glimpse in which you discover you're getting through it, is going to get longer and longer each and every day.

Because your body knows that surviving this is going to bring you a level of strength you have not yet known. I promise—" Max takes a breath, feeling with every ounce of her conviction that as she says it she'll find a way to make it true. "I promise we're going to get you not a hint, not a glimmer-of-a-pang *over him.*"

CHAPTER 16

Ben backs the van into the space he lucked into and checks to make sure he isn't too far from the curb. Hard to tell with the mound of snow that's been congealing since the Christmas storm. He cuts the engine. So not how he wants to be spending New Year's Eve. Kim thinks they're meeting up later, but he just doesn't think he feels—whatever it is he's supposed to feel at this point. What he felt with Max.

So that means he'll probably ring in the New Year at Bridget and Taylor's joint party—which is cool since Taylor's been back to his old self again. He hops out of the front seat and shuts the door, grabbing the invoice for his final delivery and double-checking the address. Crap, is this a restaurant? Why would they need a changing table? Letting out a sigh, he shoves the paper back into his pocket. The red velvet curtains covering the windows make it look like it's not even open. Whatever. He'll just leave the invoice in the door crack and head home. He's craving KFC again; maybe he'll swing by there.

Just as he's wedging the order between the handles the door opens, sending the paper to the icy pavement. Ben bends to get it and when he stands he sees Max, looking maddeningly beautiful in a red dress that seems like it was sewn to her.

Max doesn't move, her breath held as the frigid wind whips in and around her. This is her last *Teen Vogue* loan and her last hope. She's ordered about fifty items from Cooper Baby, but he's never once been the one to ferry them to her door. "Hi," she says as he stands, his cheeks pink from the cold, his eyes looking uncertain. "Thank you for coming."

"I wouldn't have," he says, "if I'd known . . ."

"But we're having a changing-table emergency."

"Luck with that." He turns back to the van. She jogs out after him.

"But I ordered it! I paid for assembly! You have to deliver it," she says gamely.

"I don't have to like it."

"Come inside," she entreats. "Don't you want to see where the table's going to be set up first? Come on, it's freezing out here."

Ben stares at her, shivering and beautiful. *And evil,* he reminds himself. *Totally freakin' evil.* "I'm not going in there with you."

"Why?"

Fuck it. "I don't trust myself."

"I'm flattered."

He goes to open the driver's door. He's got to get out of here.

"Ben, wait! You want to talk out here? Fine. I will get pneumonia to tell you this. I'm sorry. I'm so sorry. I didn't know how to tell you about any of it. That guy you saw was my ex. I honestly thought I was going to—"

"Second him?" he scoffs at her.

"What?"

"Isn't that what you do?"

"Um, Moment, you mean?"

"Whatever."

"Yes, I was going to do my Moment to clear him out of my system because I want to be with you. And I broke all my own rules and a lot of people's trust in me—"

"Including mine," Ben says simply.

Max doesn't know what to say. She knows how she

feels about him, but she didn't realize he felt that strongly back. Pushing past her shame, she reminds herself there has to be a chance here.

"I mean, at least you have that now," Ben continues, his eyes hard. "I know what it is to have my heart broken. Can I join your club?"

"I didn't mean to. I meant to do the opposite."

Ben sees her lips turning blue as her teeth chatter. But she's not moving. "Okay, look, this is sick, you're freezing. I'll go inside for two minutes. But only two. Then I need to get going."

"Thank you," she says, jogging in her thin, red heels to grab the door and hold it open for him. He's not ready for what he walks into.

Max has called in every favor to pull this off. Candles are lit, music is playing, and a tuxedoed gentleman points them to the lone table set up on the floor. Its linen cloth is littered in lush rose petals. "There was a date you offered me a little while ago and I wanted to return the favor," she says.

"And then kill me?"

"No!"

He looks down at himself. "I'm in a jumpsuit."

"I've been dreaming about that jumpsuit," she ventures bravely.

Ben looks from the table to Max, wanting to stay, to

admit he's been dreaming about a lot more than that. But—
"How do I know you're not going to hurt me again?"

"Because that's what *you* have on me now. I've learned
that hurting you feels infinitely worse than being hurt
myself. Look, have dinner with me. Even just as my
friend. Or as a passing acquaintance. Have dinner with
me as a stranger. You don't even have to talk! I'd rather sit
and not talk with you than not know you at all anymore."

He finds himself walking toward the table.

She pulls out his seat, and he lets her drape the napkin
in his lap before sitting next to him.

"Where does the changing table go?" He glances
around.

"In the kitchen. The sous chef is having twins."

"I should have brought two."

The waiter places the basket on the tablecloth and fills
their water glasses. She goes to take a piece of bread and
then doesn't. She's suddenly not sure what to do with her
hands. Where do you put your hands at a restaurant?!
"So, how was your Christmas?"

He takes the menu the waiter offers him before answering. "Um, shitty."

"Ditto." She nods.

"And your—" "I went—" They start speaking at the
same time and then smile.

"You first." She motions. "Please."

But he forgot what he was going to say. Maybe this thing between them can't be fixed.

She starts again. "Christmas?"

"My mom has a new boyfriend. And, like, six siblings. At Christmas our house is like . . . an Italian chicken coop. And I look over at my dad and I see how much he misses it all. How quiet his life is. He just seems, I don't know, stuck." Ben reaches for his water, realizing his trembling hand is audibly shaking the ice. "But I realize if I pay for school myself I'll feel better about taking the time to figure out what I really want to do with my life. So I've applied for loans and a bunch of merit scholarships."

"Wow! That's huge," Max exclaims. "Good for you."

"Thanks. He was pretty surprised that I wasn't going to Kenyon after talking his ear off about it all these years."

"You're not?"

"Nah."

"So where?" Max says, praying it's at least in this country.

"Don't know yet. Somewhere on the East Coast for sure. Somewhere I can get back home from. But I kind of needed something totally new. It's going to be really hard on my dad to have me go, no matter where I'm heading." He looks at her, an idea occurring. "Hey, this might be totally weird, but do you think you could do what you do for him, but without, like, leaving my mom shit-canned?"

"Oh! Well, we've never treated a guy, but—"

"You should consider it. Hearts are hearts."

"I'm working with my new mentor and, fingers crossed, future advisor, on an adult application of the program."

"So, you'll do it?"

She nods. "And we are reevaluating the shitcanned aspect of the program."

"I'll keep that in mind." He smiles, reminding himself to look down and figure out his order. He thinks he'll take a plate of right now followed by a dessert of more. They sit side by side in front of the flickering candelabra, the edges of their hands almost touching as they lift their menus.

Her phone starts buzzing in her clutch. "Sorry." She lunges to silence it.

"Work?" he asks, and she thinks she's lost him again. She finally fumbles it out to see a bunch of texts from her stepfather, Peter, and several missed calls.

"Something went wrong at the checkup—" Max reads hastily. "'They rushed her in for an emergency delivery. Mom and baby are fine'—oh my God! My mom had the baby!"

"What?" Ben drops his menu.

"It's a girl! A sister." She smiles at the thought for the first time. "I'm going to have a little lady to look out for!"

"Shit, I'll drive you!"

"No." Max tries to focus. "No, we're having a date. Or a stranger dinner or whatever you're up for."

"Max, let's go. We'll have our date at the hospital vending machine."

"Really?"

He takes her hand and pulls her to him, kissing her as he has been wanting to, with abandon—no longer caring about college, or his dad, or even getting hurt again.

And he needn't worry. Because just like that, she's totally and completely . . . under him.

ACKNOWLEDGMENTS

We are eternally grateful to our own Ex, Inc. team:

Farrin Jacobs, Catherine Wallace, and the entire Harper Collins staff. Suzanne Gluck, Kaye Dyja, Eve Atterman, Claudia Webb, Josh Bider, Melody Carter, Alicia Gordon, and Erin Conroy, and everyone at WMEE. Sara Bottfeld and Mahzad Babayan at Industry. Zoe Fairbourn and OpenSky. Ken Weinrib and Eric Brown. Marcy Engelman and Dana Gidney Fetayama. Claudia Ancalmo and Blair Patterson at Estée Lauder. Judy Sage, Jamie Jaffe, and Gillian Avertick at *Teen Vogue*. Tiffany Bartok. Heather, Jordana, Catherine, and everyone at Carroll Gardens All Day Preschool. Our families, especially Joel, David, Sophie, and Theo.

You've pulled us up from the floor, given us stern talking-tos, infused us with can-do spirit, and then sent us back out with songs in our hearts and smiles on our faces—on more occasions than we really care to count. Every day you make it possible for us to not-a-glimmer-of-a-shadow-of-a-doubt face the next blank page.

Thank you!

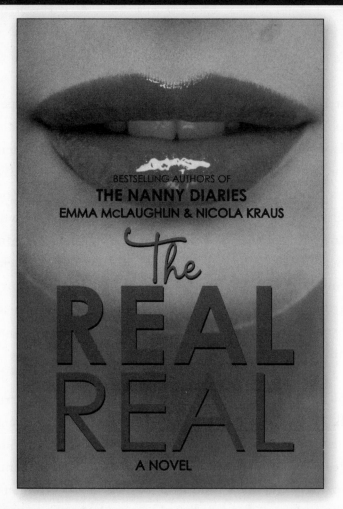